The Homeland

The Homeland

by

Hamida Na'na

by
Martin Asser

translated by
Martin Asser

Original text © 1979 Hamida Na'na.
Translation © 1995 Martin Asser.

The right of Hamida Na'na and Martin Asser to be identified respectively as the
author and translator of this work has been asserted in accordance with the
Copyright, Designs and Patents Act 1988.

First English Edition.
First published in Arabic as *Dar al-Adaab*.

Series editor: Fadia Faqir.
Literary editor: Georgina Andrewes.

ISBN: 1 85964 021 4

British Library Cataloguing-in-Publication Data.
A catalogue record for this book is available from the British Library.

Cover design by Cooper-Wilson.
Cover illustration by Peter Hay.
Typeset by Sarah Golden.
Production by Sue Coll.
Printed in Lebanon.

Ezra Pound extract reproduced from 'Ballata VIII',
The Translations of Ezra Pound with the kind permission of Faber and Faber Ltd.

Typeset in 11/13 Adobe Garamond.

Published by Garnet Publishing Ltd,
8 Southern Court, South Street,
Reading, RG1 4QS. UK.

Introduction

As an immigrant, you are usually confined to a specific space in that metaphoric country called exile. You walk around, a shadow in the background, your dreams of different homelands, your memories of torture, war and all the injustices you have suffered go almost completely undetected by the majority. I have chosen *The Homeland* for inclusion in the Arab Women Writers series, precisely because it brings the hidden history of the immigrant woman to the foreground.

Nadia, the main character in this novel, is an Arab woman living in Paris in the 1970s. She appears ordinary and nondescript yet under her Moroccan *jalaba* lies a complete history of the Palestinian resistance movement and the role of women in it. An ex-guerrilla fighter who was dismissed by the Popular Front for the Liberation of Palestine (PFLP), she is completely detached from her previous existence and passes unnoticed in Paris. To counter this she begins to set down her story, to write herself into existence.

Nadia's story and her reaction to the West also shows the resentment of the immigrants who understand themselves to be more than the host society's perception of them. "Living in Paris put the past in competition with the present . . . until the present and the past were locked up in a severe conflict. I refuse to take sides with either the East or the West. This continual conflict helps me discover and define myself."[1]

Further tension arises because Nadia is torn between her image of herself and what the traditional, tribal and conservative society perceives her to be. Her past attempts at conformity have led to her complete alienation from her true self. In an attempt to fit with her surroundings and do what she thinks is expected, she marries a famous plastic surgeon. Nadia discovers that they have different agendas and the marriage ultimately fails. That tension between the role of women as defined by society, whether eastern or western, and the role to which Nadia aspires have a severe affect on her mental health.

During this low point in her life, she meets Frank and tries to be his ideal lover, but again discovers that he is not what she wants him to be. Consequently, Nadia loses her cultural and psychological stability: an 'insect' begins to gnaw at the map of her country and her inner map. In exile, she loses her identity without gaining a new sense of wholeness, so the self begins to disintegrate since it can no longer handle or control the 'reality' around it.

While highlighting the marginalization of Nadia within a patriarchy, a position heightened by her exile, Hamida Na'na also sets out to show the ugly misogyny prevalent in Arab societies in particular. Nadia is continually discriminated against. She realizes that she speaks a different language from her male colleagues: she is interested in theoretical discussion while her 'comrades' are preoccupied with their past Arab glories. Even as a revolutionary, Nadia is disappointed with her organization. She believes that action should be centred on Palestine, that hijacking planes detracts from their main aims. Manipulated into becoming a pawn of the group's public relations vehicle, she objects and is subtly dismissed from the organization, a move which leads her to question everything she believes in.

The Homeland turns a critical face in several directions, scrutinizing the Arab world and its political organizations and the West and its repentant bourgeois revolutionaries. This latter criticism is pointed firmly at Frank. As a writer and former revolutionary, Frank has written of violent struggle in the jungles of the Congo and of armed men descending from mountains to occupy cities. Nadia is attracted to this mythical figure but Frank has changed; imprisonment in the third world has sent him running home like a prodigal son. He chooses to live in France where human rights are not violated and democracy reigns supreme. He becomes tame, joining the socialist party and starting work on a novel. Nadia realizes that the revolutionary that she had fallen in love with no longer exists and has been replaced by an establishment bourgeoisie. There is nothing to keep her in Paris and she ultimately decides to return home.

Na'na succeeds in creating two narrative lines. She shows the tensions between an individual and a political organization within the Arab countries on the one hand, contrasting this with the Arab immigrant in confrontation with an old western civilization on the other.

Much of Na'na's narrative line set in the Arab world is based on the life of Leila Khaled[2], the guerrilla fighter with the PFLP who was involved in the hijacking of TWA flight 840 from Rome to Damascus in 1969 and the attempted hijacking of an El-Al flight from Amsterdam in 1970. Khaled and Nadia have parallel experiences – like Khaled and indeed Hamida Na'na herself, Nadia is among the first women to join the Palestinian revolution and take part in military operations. Like Khaled, Nadia is a hijacker and both Khaled and Nadia undergo plastic surgery to disguise their identities. Leila Khaled and Nadia share a similar voice, they both believe in the rhetoric of Marxist-Leninist ideology, so much so that their opinions can seem simplistic or over-stated and Nadia seems to be a flat and plastic character. However she is fully rounded by the time we meet her again in Paris, where as an immigrant she suffers loneliness and invisibility and from this learns to identify herself.

The wavering of the boundaries between fiction and reality can also be seen through Nadia's influences. She has fed herself on the popular Marxist literature of Che Guevara and Fidel Castro but has been especially influenced by the writings of the French Marxist Regis Debray, a friend of the author, who was imprisoned in Bolivia from 1967–70. Debray's book *Revolution in the Revolution* became a bible for young Marxist guerrilla fighters in the Arab world. The intermingling of the characters of Frank and Debray is obvious. Nadia falls in love with Frank in Paris, thus his writings and the actual relationship make the figure of Debray omnipresent in the novel.

A further tension in this epistolary novel exists because Frank is completely unaware of Nadia's past life in the Middle East. She decides to write him a long letter telling him about the part of her life which is hidden from him, the isolation she feels because of this denial is emphasized by the separation between the present narrative line in Paris and the past narrative line of the Arab world. The parallel lines of the woman guerrilla fighter and the life of the immigrant come together at the end when Frank reads her long letter. The two lines are no longer in confrontation with each other.

The novel is written mainly in a lyrical interior monologue and in the first person. The outside reality is seen through the eyes of Nadia and the time scale is determined by her chaotic memory. The setting moves between two decades, and the cities of Paris, Aram (Damascus), Ayntab (Beirut) and Haran (Amman) to create a history absent from official accounts. The flashbacks, interior monologue, letters and dialogues seem to be disjointed, but the engagement with the question of revolution both in the Arab world and elsewhere provide the novel with structural cohesion.

Women in this series create a different language where the patriarch is lampooned and ridiculed, and where their oral and daily experiences are placed at the epicentre of the current discourse. Since the formal language excludes them, they have pushed written Arabic closer to the spoken colloquial language in order to be able to present their experiences as completely as possible. They gnaw at the foundations of the societies which marginalize them and reject traditional notions of exclusively masculine or feminine languages. From a third space within the language they represent a culture which is based on exclusion, division and misrepresentation of their religious, sexual and political experiences.

Arab women are treated as a minority in most Arab countries. They feel invisible, misrepresented and reduced. It is therefore vital that they be heard. In the absence of many good translators from Arabic to English, a problem partly responsible for the lack of Arab cultural intervention in the international arena, Martin Asser's translation is significant.

Now I invite the reader to open the book of Arab women's 'meta-culture'. This book is part of a secular project, challenging the foundations of a patriarchal, tribal system. If you lift this double-layered veil, you will see the variant, colourful and resilient writings of Arab women, the fresh inner garden. You will also hear the clear voices of Arab women singing their survival.

Fadia Faqir
Durham, 1995

1. This quotation is taken from *In the House of Silence: Conditions of Arab Women's Narratives*, Fadia Faqir, ed., a collection of testimonies by Arab women novelists to be published by Garnet Publishing to complement this series.
2. For more information on Leila Khaled please read *My People Shall Live: The Autobiography of a Revolutionary*, ed., George Hajjar, Hodder and Stoughton, London, 1973.

You know it is wartime.

Death-time. Time for conflagrations and far off lands. Time for vagrancy on the streets of exile. Time to be spent in strange cities, their faces clothed in the mist. All links to your distant homeland are broken. Only alienation remains. You gaze in the mirror and watch the woman in front of you dying slowly day by day, and the child within her blood being awakened.

You know it is wartime.

War and time. The night always brings you back to that bitter reality. You try to obliterate yourself, hurling yourself against the pavements of loneliness. You hear the sound of your voice issuing from your throat and echoing to you emptily from the thin air. The ink has ceased to attract you. The blank sheets of paper have lost that bewitching lustre. The keen urge to confess your secret is dulled.

Where will you go?

The town which you normally pass through, carrying the grand dream of return in your head, has become a prison. The wild jujube trees stick into the heart of your misfortune before vanishing under the pressure of the wind.

Night, why can't you stop your chatter?

Why can't you smother yourself in the gloom, and let me rest?

Since when have I felt anything for the pavement cafés, or for the faces of strangers? Or for these pavements which are soaked in the blood of my comrades? Or for the sense of failure which plunges me back into the depths of myself, vanquished? The time has come to be a woman again.

I know it is wartime.

I know that it is also the time for rebirth. The time for trees seen in that hot Mediterranean country, each one clasping her daughter branches to her body, so that loneliness dies within her. But the branches must also die, since to soothe herself she crushes the life out of them.

I come from a land where everything dies at the moment of its birth, and where everything lives in its own death. I come from a land where the heavens pour water into the earth for a hundred days, and where the sun draws the waters back up into the heavens for many hundreds more.

That is where I come from, a place where war still teems at the source of every river.

I know it is wartime.

And I know that it is also the time of failure, and defeat, and surrender. And a time for questions which burn in my throat and echo from the abyss without being answered.

The time for nameless fears and endless waiting.

Paris, 1977 – I run towards you feeling the rain beating against my face and my body. I see the snow dancing in front of the bridges linking the Ile de la Cité to the old town.

Pulling my Moroccan cloak around me, I push forward into the darkness. You are standing under a riverside shelter by a street lamp. The mist eddies around you, like the music of gypsies coming up from valleys of joy. I approach:

"Sorry I'm late. My boss kept on giving me more work to do. I am always telling him that he has to let me go on time. Six o'clock means freedom as far as I'm concerned." I laugh, then carry on: "But he's Arab of course, so he has a bit of trouble knowing what 'on time' means!"

"I shouldn't worry about it," you reply with a smile. "Look what we did with time over here. Three world wars, God knows how many other local conflicts."

Stretching your hand out towards me, you start stroking my rain-soaked hair. Then you shelter me under your leather jacket and we set off towards the Place Dauphine. I stop on the Quai des Orfèvres opposite the Palais de Justice and look up at you. I cannot see you properly through the storm but, amidst the wind and rain, you look like a ship's captain, undertaking an endless voyage without so much as a single stop at port. I say to you:

"Two world wars. And we're fighting a cause against hopeless odds . . . Sometimes I wish another war would start; at least we would know where we stood then."

I see a cloud of anger pass across your face. You have many different expressions and I can never quite tell what each one of them signifies. I feel you leaning on me a little more, trying to hug me.

"Don't be so stupid. You know it's crazy to think like that."

Talking about war means delving into your past; talking about the Arab world means going into mine . . . my present too, I suppose. Whenever I look at maps of the region everything has changed. Towns getting bigger or smaller, territories being called by other names, even the passports have changed colours.

At the entrance to your building, we both look at the face of the Algerian cook in the restaurant next door. He is singing that song which makes me think back to the past and all its wounds. How I long to forget! I try to get close to you and to say to myself that we are here to erase the past.

We climb the steps leading to the wooden staircase up to your flat. I rest against you, trying to forget that face. We listen to our footsteps on the ancient wooden boards. Both of us look at the nameplate on the door of the first-floor flat. The name belongs to one of France's leading actresses. I smile and repeat the first part of it. Then I stop and turn towards you:

"Frank, isn't she . . . "

You do not let me finish the question.

"That's enough! She's French, and that's that."

A wave of anger hits me and I become determined to finish what I was going to say. You look at me beseechingly, as though I have touched a wound which is festering in your body.

I get very stubborn in moments of resolve, however. It is as though the whole world is welling up inside me, ready to burst out whenever I want it to. This has afforded me a certain self-possession in my life, verging on narcissism, even at the moments of great danger which my life has seen. I wait until we have passed the door on which we read the name and have turned to go to the second floor. Then I lean against the wall and say:

"She's Jewish, isn't she?"

You have a lot of trouble with the way I measure the world. A frown comes across your face and you put your hand on my shoulder, saying:

"That's all there is as far as you're concerned, isn't it: Arabs and Jews. Can't you put all that behind you?"

I remain silent, but a voice inside me says, No . . . Not if you are nursing a wound like mine. No.

We listen to the River Seine outside. Through the window on the stairway it mixes with the sound of the rain. There are no explosions . . . no blood . . . no screams. What a dump Paris is!

When we get to your flat, I take off my cloak by the front door and reach for the towel hanging on the wall. I wrap up my long hair and squeeze out the drops of rainwater.

"Why do you start laughing every time I ask why you came here? I know about your studies, your job, your husband, and all of that; but what exactly made you choose Paris?"

You put this question to me as you are sitting down on the sofa overlooking the river.

"I've told you everything. I came here with my husband, and started studying after that. When we split up I decided to stay on a bit . . . before going back home."

"Do you want to go back?"

"Very much."

"What have you got back there?"

"What did you have back in France? I've read your memoirs. While you were in prison you became a perfect Frenchman."

You wince and I feel you did not want to be reminded of that time. You always try to avoid conversations about your past, as though those far-off days were no longer anything to do with you.

"In prison I used to dream of the Ile de la Cité and remember the trees in the parks of Paris. It seemed to me that I knew them all, each and every one. . . . "

Two years have passed since your return to France. You came back wishing to atone and to forget. Four years you spent in prison, under the scorching sun in that far-off land . . . One of those 'Third World' countries, as they say in your language.

"Why did you go there in the first place, then?"

"What is this? A newspaper interview?"

"Frank, if only you knew how curious I am about your past. I'd read all your books by the age of eighteen. It was your books which kindled my enthusiasm and turned me into a defender of your theories of revolution."

"You still don't understand, do you?"

"What do you mean?"

"I mean that what I wrote back then was an adventure. And I have paid for it dearly. Please, let's talk about something else. I don't like talking about myself. Can't we talk about you?"

"You know about me already."

And I say no more. In fact you know almost nothing about me. You only know about Nadia the student, who showed up one day at the École Normale Supérieure to attend a lecture you gave about the revolutionary movement, whose black hair and gypsy features caught your eye, who had an affair with you. It was your notoriety which drew me to you, and I began an adventure the outcome of which I could never have foreseen.

Paris. January, 1976. Six o'clock in the evening.

I entered the lecture hall accompanied by a journalist friend of mine who came from one of the countries which were the scenes of your exploits. We were driven there by a desperate curiosity to see the last throes of this professional revolutionary.

"Have you heard? He's going to be speaking at the École Normale tonight. I wonder what he's got to say for himself?"

That is what my companion had said to me while he was talking about you. I had followed the wave of vituperation which you were subjected to in the media and among the political parties here and in the country that you had left. Like all decent people, my friend still believed in proletarian revolution in Europe and the rest of the world – well, we can always dream can't we? All kinds of things had been said about you:

"A spoiled brat who, when he found he could not keep up the struggle, leapt back into the arms of the bourgeoisie."

"Europe has taken back what it spat out onto the stage of World Revolution."

"The deaths of many of our comrades can be attributed to his confessions."

Such were the latest insults directed at you in the press. At the time I was a bit lost and depressed, trying to patch up my life again after the split with my husband. The man I married had chosen his own well-being and had left me with my inner homeland in flames. He had grown sick of my eternal see-saw from oblivion to memory and back again.

I come from the East . . .

I come from a land which was ablaze the last time I saw it. My comrades were facing the moment of death with no thought of ease or comfort in their heads. But I chose to flee to Europe. I gave in to the over-stuffed bellies, the sense of well-being, the inner woman. That's what my comrades thought and that's what I believed myself.

Why am I doing this to myself? I didn't choose to come here at all. I was forced to come because I needed to get away from them for a while. I needed a rest. But there is an open wound in my side. There are jet fighters overhead in a deep blue sky. There are men's bodies lying on the ground. I am a prisoner of the past. It takes me back to those towns which have been thrown into the fire to burn.

"Has it ever occurred to you that our relationship is not on an even footing?"

"What do you mean?"

"Well, you know everything about me and I know nothing about you. You can read all my books and you can understand everything I say, but you could be writing about anything for all I know. Do you still write poetry?"

I laugh:

"You'd better learn Arabic then, hadn't you!"

You stretch out on the sofa and stare up at the ceiling:

"Do you think I could?"

"Have a go."

"But I'm forty now, and I'm looking for an easy life."

It was on cold evenings like this that we used to meet one another. Cold evenings are the best times for the coming together of a man and a woman. Their bodies feel the need for warmth and their souls have had enough of the rain.

And now?

September sun has dried up all the rain. I am alone and you are far away. But my soul is awake once more.

We spent a year of our lives together. It was a year ago that you left your house, your wife, your daughter, and moved in with me in your new lodgings over the road from the Palais de Justice. The experiment of our living together was begun.

"Frank, I can't stand it when I think of your wife and what she might be going through."

"What makes you think she is going through anything. We were together for fourteen years, you know. We're just good friends now."

I leave you in the gloom of the view of the river and move through to the sitting-room. I glance around at the piles of newspapers and magazines from various parts of the world: *Nouvelle Critique, Cars of America, Afrique-Asie*. Languages without dates. On the wall are maps of the world, distant continents surrounded by oceans of silence. The painting of an old Spanish sailor sitting on a God-forsaken coastline looks to me like Hemingway's old man of the sea. I once remarked to you that it reminded me of something done by our painter friend Césire.

"Don't be ridiculous! The only things Césire can paint are Chilean sunsets and Mexican girls with big brown eyes!"

My insistence on it being a Césire made you so irritated that you took the picture down from the wall one day, and gave me a long lecture about the Belgian artist, Delfoe, who had painted it. That day I said to you, quite simply:

"I don't care who painted it. That face looks like one of Césire's, especially with that strange look in his eyes. And the sun, like a brown disc in the sky without any light or warmth."

It was the first time I had seen a sun which did not actually shine, not that it matters, I suppose.

You told me about a country where the sun rises for a long time and goes on shining as it dies. You told me:

"I used to pray for rain there. In the dungeons of torture, with my body soaked in my own blood, I prayed for my return to France. I prayed for my body to cleave to one of the columns of Paris and for it to stay there for ever. I built the dome of the Panthéon in my mind and I mapped out the streets of Paris around it. My fondest dream was that one day I would once again be able to drink a cup of coffee on the Boulevard Saint Germain."

"It seems as though you don't want to have anything to do with your past. I am surprised by that. If you haven't already forgotten it, then you are trying hard to forget that once you were the very embodiment of the dreams and hopes of a whole generation."

"They made me into a legend! I couldn't stand that."

I turn my head away so you can't see the tears coming to my eyes. It is hard not to cry at moments like these, when I have to ask myself what I am doing with you.

I tell myself that the struggle has failed. Even Frank has lost faith. I go to the shower in the hope that the hot water will wash away the memories of my comrades. But within me, behind the layers of deceit, there is a secret which cannot be erased, which never ceases to torture me, which never lets me go. A retired guerrilla fighter, looking to forget in the company of another who has already forgotten.

I was on the way to being an ordinary woman again before I met you. I would eat, sleep and make love by night, and then I would go off to work in the morning. That way I thought I could live and forget . . .

My husband used to say:

"I don't think you'll ever forget. The picture of Huda al-Shafi'i follows you wherever you go. Why can't you just live an ordinary life?"

When my husband said that, I would stare down at the ground. I can still see their faces when they left me to go to their deaths.

Frank! You mustn't forget!

The evening hangs over the Place Dauphine. You are standing on the corner waiting for me. Darkness creeps out of the night, plunging me into the pits of alienation and oblivion. I go towards you. I put my head on your chest and smell your skin. You stroke my hair then put your arm around me. We walk together under the glow of the street-lights which are scattered about the heart of Paris. We pass along Boulevard Saint Honoré. We stand and look into the shop windows. Then we move on, as though the life of this dyspeptic city does not really concern us.

"I am leaving for Africa tomorrow. I have been asked to take part in a Revolution Day celebration there."

I had forgotten that you were a piece of their history. I had forgotten that it was you who, once upon a time, had set light to their cities. Weren't you just like any other man, not the great revolutionary. I gave myself up to you because you were trying to forget them, just as I was.

"Will you be away for a long time?"

"A month at least. Why don't you come with me?"

"You must be joking. You know perfectly well that I can't just leave my job here in Paris. I'll wait for you."

"Yes, do wait for me. Even if you are not faithful, please wait."

I look at you with surprise:

"Frank, I shall be myself."

At that moment we were crossing the Place du Châtelet on the way to your flat. At the point where the Boulevard des Orfèvres meets Saint Michel bridge, I saw an Arab friend of mine in the crowd. I ran after him without really seeing where he was going. You followed me with a mixture of surprise and curiosity. You didn't think that Europe had turned me into a block of ice too, did you?

The following day saw us standing outside the departure gate at Charles de Gaulle Airport. We were looking at each other and trying to seem closer than we really felt. I heard them call your flight. I don't know why but I had this strange feeling that this would be the last time we would see each other. I stared at the faces of the other pass-engers bustling along the walk-ways. We remembered that the time for us to part had arrived. I tried to think of something to say to you, before your departure, but the words failed me. First I muttered something incomprehensible and then I managed to say: "I'll be waiting for you."

Frank!

That was a month ago now Frank, and you have not called me. You have not sent me a card with a picture of the local fighters, with you in the middle.

At this moment, I feel myself drawn towards the lights of Pont-Neuf and the Ile de la Cité. I see a ghost in one of the shelters by the Place Dauphine where we used to meet. For a moment I think it is your ghost. The wind blows against my heart and the papers which I have clutched to my breast.

"Why haven't you come back?"

My tormented cry is heard by a night-watchman, who turns round and looks at me with desire mingled with suspicion. I quicken my pace across the paving stones of the bridge. I hear your voice calling from far away and whispering within me. It says: "Be yourself, and nothing but yourself." In moments of weakness, the alienation of people like me, people who are away from home, makes it impossible for them to dream.

I've had enough!

Do I love you?

I am not sure. All I can think about now is my wound. I think bitterly that I am living in a time of war, and that peace (your favourite subject) is nothing more than a lie which man has to believe in so that he can go on living. I suddenly remember that I cannot go home – that I have buried my past in the fabric of those old walls. It is a past which torments me and which will not leave me alone whatever I am doing.

I remember, but I am trying to forget, and there is a present which exists only in my head. I am alone and I have no weapons except the wounds which inhabit my body.

I told you about it. I told you that there is a dagger within me, that somewhere in my body is a deep and lasting rupture which could kill me at any moment, that I have this open wound which is getting deeper by the day and the deeper it gets, the more important it becomes to forget.

The wound. The woman and the homeland banished in her head. Abu Mashour. You. The journeys of madness into the lands of silence and exile.

The wound.

I can feel the dagger going deeper. I can hear the blood surging through my veins, mixing with the sound of the River Seine. I feel sick. I feel that I cannot go on any longer. I want to give myself a few moments before it is all over to tell you about the wound. I go towards a café beside the shelter where we used to meet. I stroll inside and put my cloak over one of the chairs. I spread my papers out over the table. I breathe in the warm smell. A woman, who always sits at one of the corner tables, looks up at me from the book which she has been reading for months now, a detective story – maybe she reads it over and over again and puts herself in the position of the heroine, or one of the characters who plays a major role in the plot.

Do you remember that time when you pointed her out to me and said:

"How sad it is when we finish up reading novels in cafés. We place all the troubles and failures of this life in them, and then we look for words, for things which might bring our relationship with this world back to life."

I look at that woman's face and I see you in thirty years' time. The controversy surrounding you would have long since died down, and the papers would no longer be publishing stories about you. You will be sitting at a corner table of an old café, one of those on the Ile de la Cité, reading over everything you have written in your life and dreaming of the heroes of your stories. This thought makes me shiver, and I think of all the towns of the Arab World, the sun which does not leave us to be alone, and the wind which does not come to an accord with us.

I once said to you:

"Frank! It must be horrible to grow old in this country. Being alone here is unbearable."

You replied:

"It's worse when you can't find solitude."

Your answer did not convince me. That day I told you about my father and mother, about their long running arguments which surely would have led to their divorce were it not for their nine children whom they had brought into this world in a few fleeting moments of love.

I think of their faces for a few moments. I try to find a little love in my heart for them. But all that I feel is my banishment from them and from the far-off land where they are living.

Father, where is your face in this night? Where are your hands, which you withdrew from me for my own protection? And you, my mother, I want to tell you that . . .

I told you about the long nights I spent in a town overlooking the Mediterranean Sea. I told you about the sea, the hours I spent gazing at the sea. I told you that it is the colour of the night, but you did not believe me.

"Everyone knows what colour the sea is. It's blue."

I feel like a mischievous child trying to make excuses when she has said something wrong:

"But listen, the sea can be all kinds of different colours. Sometimes I thought I must be drunk, and that was before I had ever had a drink."

You told me the story of the drunks who thought they were supermen and could move mountains as though they were chess pieces.

"Don't you know anything about the history of the Gauls?"

"No not really, and I fail to see why you have such great faith in them."

"Don't be silly. Anyway, its not about faith."

I was trying to be completely clear about what I meant when I told you about the sea and about my mother and father. I was trying to replenish the springs of the desire to belong which had dried up inside me. I am standing on a street corner opposite the Café Fleur. My forehead pressed against the wall of an old church. In my mind's eye you stand beside me on the stone pavement. That is how Paris is now, in the last hour of the night.

A month has passed since your departure and I am just beginning to wake up again. I began to see that my stay here is only temporary and that I will not be here for ever. I still harbour the dream that one day I shall be returning to the land which I left on that dusty morning with the sun beating down onto my brow.

A month has passed since your departure, and I am just beginning to realize that the years I have spent here trying to forget have all been in vain. Before I first got to know you, I had built an impregnable strong-hold against my memories.

But four years, that is my limit. Now it is time to launch myself again into the world outside. Now is the time to reassess my life. That is the survival instinct . . . I have to risk my life in order to save it . . . before I met you, Frank, I would look to men and knowledge and the echoes of history, and they would help me. Althussen, Goldman. Shar. Suddenly I realized that my actions were just another part of my fear of death, or rather my fear of life. I said to you before you departed:

"Why don't you just turn down this invitation to go there?"

"I feel I'm getting old here. I need a change of scenery. I thought that I would be just an ordinary person in my own land, not some expert, just an ordinary citizen who wanted to live his life in peace."

"But you are what you are, Frank. Even here, you will never just be an ordinary citizen."

And that day you asked me: "What about you?"

"Me? . . . I am a person who wants to look for her blood over there . . . and who has forgotten to search for it here . . . I have retired in the world of a man, and here I am going back again to the world to look for a more just situation."

"If you are so keen on democracy, tell me why it never seems to work in the Middle East?"

I looked down at the pavement and thought about the women of the Arab world carrying the heads of their husbands and sons under their arms. How long will they bide their time before they can have their revenge?

"It is not as simple as that. The way I see it, the only way to solve the problems of the Middle East is revolution."

"What do you mean, 'revolution'?"

"It's what you used to talk about all those years ago, Frank. Sowing the seeds of revolt around the world."

"But can't you see. That's just not possible any more. Look at the map of the world. I used to be a dreamer, but now I've realized that although humanity can live by its dreams it can also die from them."

We were driving along Rue Beaunier towards the University Campus. Suddenly we decided to turn around and head out of Paris. We were beset by a feeling of claustrophobia and so we drove out to your house in the country. Dusk was falling as we crossed the fertile Normandy plains.

We were getting close to Honfleur. It was getting dark over the Channel and we could see the sailing boats returning to the harbour. The fragrant night air entered the car. Your hands were beginning to loosen their grip on the steering wheel. I put my head on your shoulder and for a few minutes I felt at ease. I heard you speaking in the distance. There seemed to be a slight constriction in your throat which made your voice sound like church bells sounding a death knell.

"One evening the commandant came to see me and told me to get my things ready. I was going to be moved to another prison. I had spent two years in that prison. In solitary confinement. I was not allowed to associate with the other prisoners. My right to receive visits from the outside had long since been withdrawn. My body was just beginning to get back some of its vigour after they had finished having their fun with it. I kept telling myself that I was going to be executed. Each time I was transferred to another prison, I would sit in the office of the head of general intelligence with his assistants and the American 'advisers' and the interrogations would start all over again: How did you enter the country? Who was your contact? Who was there with you the day they advanced on the capital? Every time my answers were recorded afresh. All attempts to have me released made by the French Embassy had failed. The public campaign calling for my freedom failed too. I had been pronounced guilty and I was sentenced to life imprisonment. I began to see how good the world outside looked from behind the bars of a prison cell. The simple pleasures of walking along the Quai des Orfèvres, the sad face of my girlfriend, the voice of Abile, my mentor. I realised that I did not want to rot away behind the walls of a cell, and I wanted to go back to living my life so that I could see them all again.

"I had got quite used to the guard's face outside my cell, coming towards me out of the darkness. I would miss that if I was moved on. We'd just begun to see eye to eye with one another over the last few weeks. The new military regime had started to open up to progressive forces outside the country and this had meant that I received a bit more contact with people. I had become used to the faces of my guards and executioners, the walls of my room and the ink-stained wooden table. The guard would talk to me about the drought which had swept through the country, and how it made life difficult and had caused an economic crisis. From time to time I would have the luxury of reading a page or two from the local newspapers which he managed to smuggle in for me. I was not looking forward to the prospect of giving up this relative comfort and going to a new cell and a new executioner.

"He said to me, while he was helping me to put my books into a bag:

"'Well, Monsieur Frank, I hope they set you free this time. I think you've had enough of all this.'

"They blindfolded me and put me in a jeep. Several hours later the blindfold was taken off and I found myself in the office of the intelligence chief. There he was. He hadn't changed a bit. The only difference was that he was by himself this time, without his American advisers.

"'We are going to set you free today. I hope that we never see your face again in our land.'

"I had nothing to say to them. Although I have decided not to go back to that country, I shall fight against fascism wherever I find it. I remembered the words of Abile, as he was saying goodbye to me before I left them in the jungle which hemmed in the capital city:

"'Go home and tell them about our struggle, Frank. There are plenty of people to fight for our cause here. Go back to where the people know who you are and aren't wondering what you are doing among them. Go back to where the only thing you'll get asked is where you come from and what your family name is.'

"In the darkness of that morning I was driven through the streets of the capital in an army truck. The French military attaché was allowed to go with me to the airport. He was there to discuss where it would be best for me to go onto from there. Without hesitating I told him that I wanted to go to Paris."

I look at you. The sweat is pouring down your forehead. In the light of the street lamps, spread out on each side of the road leading to Honfleur, your eyes wander like two pools of mercury.

As I listened I tried to treat you with quiet tenderness. I did not want to ask you too many questions. Prisoners do not like to be reminded of their experiences. I tried to escape from the memory of my own past in my homeland and the period of my life when I travelled from city to city searching for justice for a people who live out their exile in despair.

You stopped the car at your garden gate and we both got out. My mind was far away from you; far from the Channel far, from Honfleur, town of the Impressionists. I was slipping back to the east, to my days of hardship. I was trying to understand your past and your current desire to distance yourself from areas of danger, and to choose your safety.

Light streamed in to us from the lamps in the garden. I lay down and sprawled on the wooden floor of the sitting-room. I stared at the ceiling and listened to the noise of the sea which was raging outside. It was louder than the wind which tore through the silence of the trees outside. I did not know what the time was. I tried to search a little in my memory for something other than the present time which we were living, but all I could think of was the company of my comrades and my days in the east, in Ayntab which was ablaze. The lights of Ayntab were mingled in my memory with the sound of the waves breaking on the shore. You were sitting at a table in the corner writing something. Every now and then you looked at me with your wandering eyes.

My body was weak and my mind filled with questions ever since I had heard the dreadful news of Mary-Rose. She had been shot crossing a checkpoint in Ayntab three days previously. But why? And who had done it? I ask you if you know anything about it, and you say: "Mary-Rose? Who's Mary-Rose? The world is full of Mary-Roses."

She had been my comrade-in-arms in the last European operation and now she was lying dead in Ayntab. Well, maybe she wasn't dead yet, but she soon would be.

"Was she a Palestinian?"

"She was a Palestine-Lebanese, but she came from Syria."

"No, I mean was she with the Palestinians?"

"Why else do you think they seized her? Because she was whistling after dark?"

"And you? Do you know her? What's made you think of her now?"

"Yes, I knew her. We were together . . . "

Immediately after I said that, I remembered that I was not meant to talk about my past life. I have made a promise never to do so. A cloud of sorrow filled my head. Mary-Rose dead. My contempt for Europe was reawakened and I longed to be back there.

You raise your head from your books and papers, your world of words. You escape for a while from the monotonous strings of letters, the monotony of the moment itself:

"Tell me, is it true what they say about the Palestinian leaders?"

"What about them particularly?"

"Oh you know, their links with certain reactionary organisations, the fantastic wealth they have accumulated, the way they stand in the face of national unity. . . . "

The great tragedy is laughing, spitting out blood. I don't know what to say to you.

"I really don't want to get into that sort of thing right now, if you don't mind."

You do not stray from your work for too long. You are drawn back into the world of words and phrases and fictions, those things that have replaced real action for you. You immerse yourself in your papers again. I go on with my inner struggle. Why don't you ask me about my life? Why doesn't suspicion and certainty drive you to pierce through the layers of deceit, to look further than the face of the woman you love and to see the woman-tree behind the mask? The time passes as I lie on the wooden floor looking up at the sky coming in from the window. I see my life with you as a temporary stop-over on my way back to the East. I see Mary-Rose's blood over your books and papers, over the windows of your bedroom. Rose-red blood stopping joy and history moving forward through time. Where am I? What am I doing here? Let me go back a little. Let me go back to my previous life.

Who am I?

A voice assails me every minute of every day. It eats away at my complacency and my ease. It makes me think back to a small town by the sea where I was born. My father was once an officer in the occupying French army. A veil of pride crosses his countenance at the mention of his Kurdish origins. I feel suffocated by this veil and sometimes I want to cry out:

"Look, I speak Arabic. I was born here. I don't know anything else."

From there, with the sea lying silently to one side and the mountains waiting close by on the other, I learn to draw the map of the world, starting at the Gulf of Alexandretta. It is a world without boundaries. I learn at school that Palestine is close and that it only takes a short trip by boat to get there. As I grow up, however, I begin to learn the whole truth . . . The way to Palestine passes through the heart of all the towns of the Arab World. My father takes pride in his ancestors who liberated Jerusalem. He takes pride in his lineage to Salah ad-Din and the noble Kurdish dynasties. He is always reminding me of my elevated origins:

"You're a princess. Your blood is not like anyone else's. You must hold your head up, even when your face is in the dust. You're a princess and you must never forget it."

My imagination is set alight and in my dreams I ride a white stallion over foaming salt waters which seem to go on for ever. But I am approaching the point where the line is drawn between the sea and the land.

On the Isle of Arwad the King of Egypt did bathe with his mistress.

Time passes, bringing wind and rain to the town by the sea. The pasture and the pine trees awaken. In my fifteenth year I meet a teacher who has come to us from Arum. Her language is filled with words like 'Freedom' and 'the People.' She talks to me about 'justice'. She tells me about a political party whose aim it is to redraw the plan of those Arab towns. One day she says to me:

"You can join us if you like."

I was young when I joined them. I was young when I learnt that I had comrades everywhere on the map of the Arab lands and that they were fighting against a bitter reality and, they like me, dreamt of the sweeter time which was coming . . . I was young when I made Palestine my dream and when I learnt about the massacres of Deir Yasin and Jerusalem.

What sadness for that fourteen-year-old girl now that she knows what has happened since those days! The years have gone by. Time has not stood still. Freedom and Palestine are still nothing more than distant dreams.

I remember my weekly meetings with my comrades. we would turn the words into shining stars. With our hands trembling by our sides we would repeat the slogans and doctrines of the party to one another over and over again. I did not tell my father or mother about these meetings and so I began to live a life of furtiveness and secrecy. I was living with a strange feeling which I made sure would never see the light of day. By night I would secretly read the party literature, and assimilate and memorise what I had read. Then, in the early hours, under the cover of darkness I would go out into the streets and distribute the pamphlets to the houses of my comrades. In all weathers, at all times of day or night and in all seasons, I would be going from house to house and from street to street around the town. The country was living under tyranny during that period and if I had been caught, I would have been in serious trouble. The eyes of the police were everywhere, but I was living my adventure.

One day the teacher tells me: "You must be careful. If your family were to find out it would be a disaster. And if the authorities get wind of what you're doing, you'll be put in prison."

I was not frightened by either my family or the police. I was with my comrades and we were waiting for tomorrow. I have been waiting since I was fourteen, and tomorrow has still not come. My journey has been a long one, passing through the cities of the north and the poems of Sulaiman al-'Issa, the music which gave life to his words. I make my first attempts at writing down my poetry. Words, words which lead to the colour of snow and the days to come.

With my father again. The names of his ancestors, their pictures on the walls. His blue blood. The princes who sired him and placed him on this earth. With my father again, speaking about the homeland of his people and their dignity. He spoke about the mountain range which was their home and those members of the family who were still living there. Not a word of all that interests me now. What did they know about the poems of Sulaiman al-'Issa or the Baghdad Uprising?

Little by little I grow up. I turn my face to the town and my eyes reflect its bright lights. My mother tells me about a wealthy man who is desirous of marrying me. She promises me riches, spacious mansions, countless trips to Europe. She tells me about an overheated house and the smell of a man gorged on wealth. I think of my three sisters, each of whom has ended up in a big house with a man whose features are just like those of my father. I remember them being turned into beautiful, silky-skinned, baby factories. I refused. I said no. I clung to my books and my studies to save me from this approaching stranger. My mother could not believe it:

"What is wrong with you? You won't have to lift a finger. He'll just shower you with money."

On summer evenings I close my windows, and write down words which I have been carrying in my head the whole day and which have become so heavy that I can hardly bear them any more. Love poetry. Poems about Palestine. Plans for a new homeland, a new party. I breathe life into men. The words become too small to hold the dream. I fall into the dream and wait.

"One day you will be a great poet."

So the teacher had said when I showed her some of my work. My mother scoffs at the teacher's words:

"Poetry is folly. You're much too sensible for that sort of thing. You're a princess and you should never forget that. Now you'll be the wife of the richest man in town and the mother of his children."

From that day I felt only disgust for the rulers, lords and princes. I search for a path which is as far away as possible from them and I find it in the Sa'alik poets, the vagabonds of pre-Islam, whose blood was shed with impunity by the Arab tribes. I am one of them. I belong to the kingdom of the Sa'alik, and one day my blood will be free to spill. I reject them all: the rulers, the lords and the princes.

The rich stranger comes to our house and promises me joy, happiness and wealth. I watch the words being belched up from his stomach and dispersed around the room like the lies they are. "No one owns tomorrow! All the money in the world wouldn't induce me to marry you and have your children."

The rich stranger takes his leave. My mother is distraught and tears come to her eyes. My father rages at me:

"What do you think you are doing? Do you want to drag our faces in the mud? You are going to get married and that is that."

A storm passes through the big house surrounded by palm trees.

My brothers start shouting:

"She's mad! It'll be a scandal on the whole family."

One of them grabs my long hair and starts to hit my head against the wall. The blood flows past my eyes. It is a pure, red colour. So my father was lying the day he said it was blue. I fall ill. My body will not tolerate this treatment. I wait days, months, a whole year. I leave home. I go to Arum to complete my higher education. At last I am out of their clutches. I remember Arum, the party which I created in my mind, in stark contrast with the unfamiliar faces of my new comrades in the party of which I am a member. I devote my life to long hours of reading and learning about the past, about philosophy and history. I see myself throughout the passing of the years and I live my daily life in expectation for the time to come.

I get letters from my mother which are full of reprimands and exhortations. My father's letters mainly contain pleas for me to steer clear of men and preserve my virginity until I come back home. My brothers come and visit me – to make certain their honour is not being compromised, no doubt. University life is all about failure and disappointment, about brave revolutionary words, about tomorrow. About poetry too.

Arum makes a poet of me, screaming with the injustices done to me through the years, and the repression which has afflicted my nation. It makes a woman of me, a woman who loves her man and waits for him. I meet comrades in the party and I talk to them about the truth which is our people. I say to them: "You are just a bunch of future tyrants dreaming about the high-ranking positions which you'll get, and the fast cars you'll drive." I tell them: "The party which we created in our hearts and minds bears no relation to you lot. Don't talk to me about the masses. What do you know about the masses?" They sneer and turn their backs on me. More proclamations are issued. More of their lies clutter up the walls of the town. I see the mouth of the abyss getting wider, preparing to swallow us all up. I write about their isolation, about the doubts which they have about the masses, about the mistakes which they make on a daily basis. The walls go up between them and me. They end up not being able to stand my presence, while I cannot bear to be with them.

At night I search for the dreams which populated my life in the town by the sea. I search for my intellectual fathers. I search for the vast poems which I used to live for and which once pierced the veil of rain and mist, the veil of night and dictatorship. However, it becomes clear to me that while the dream is one thing, reality is a different thing altogether.

My failure and frustration drags me into the cafés of Arum and Ayntab where the intellectuals gather. Through the smoke and whisky fumes, our voices talk revolution. The words are carried up in the smoke. The dreams fall back into our glasses. Our brave cries are lost in verses of nonsense poetry. The fire in our bodies is extinguished. At the end of the night we all pour out onto the streets singing about the pain of separation in the sentimental Iraqi love-song, "Firagik sa'b, ya Hawaya."

We were waiting for war, but we were never actually expecting it to happen. Then in June, 1967 . . .

I search for a gun, for fire, for a knife, for anything which might repulse them at the gates of Arum.

There was no gun. No fire. No knife.

The defeat comes. I am out in the open while aeroplanes hurl down their bombs onto men, women and children, onto the streets, into our very hearts. A knife was buried deep in our breasts. The blood was black this time. Once again my father was proven a liar. How could he have thought that blood was the colour of happiness?

1967. The year of defeat. I am torn to pieces. I am just one of the multitude whose bodies had been weakened by being stabbed over and over again. I am just a poet, one of the coffee-house intelligentsia, who is staring her defeat in the face and who is unable to do anything to stop it. The noise of aircraft rips through the silence of our days. I can see the world in its entirety. Everything has changed. Aeroplanes rain fire down on Arum. All the maps and charts become merged together in my mind and I see a single front-line which has been overrun by the enemy. Another wave of immigrants arrives. We call them 'immigrants' – who am I to disagree with what it says in the dictionary?

I go to my comrades in the party and I try to make them remember. What is the use of memory though? What is the use of tears? Everything will be consumed in our wounds. Words die in the lines of poems, poetry itself dies in the pits of despair. Heroes fall from their heroic deeds. The masks are torn away. We are all displayed under the fire of defeat, helpless and enchained. The days pass and our wounds heal, but we shall never forget.

I remember 1967. Lying there, ripped to shreds, one of the vanquished millions, a coffee-house intellectual, the stifled cries of protest in my throat. An artists' and writers' conference was convened in Cairo, a self-styled 'Conference of Resistance.' They could hardly have come up with a less appropriate title.

I remember it well. A hall at the Faculty of Arts ringing with our empty phrases. We consumed the words as fast as they were consuming us. Our poetry now looked like an old woman's face stripped of her make-up. Our different political affiliations were a picture of the crisis which faced our nation. Injustice was stamped on the brow of every one of the true fighters. The prisons had torn through the hearts of many people for many years.

Meetings and speeches. Meetings and poetry recitals. Meetings where we curse the political organisations. But in the face of each person there, you can see those very politicians and those very organizations. You can see both the killer and the victim. We are seen for what we really are. Our dream leads us only to nothingness. The official writers are all there, the pet writers of the organisations, still with their villas and their fat salaries. They are unaffected by the failures and they do not seem to be feeling the slightest embarrassment. Sometimes I feel so disgusted that I have to leave the hall. I head towards an old bar near the University. I sit there with a glass in my hand. Drink was the only hero after the Fifth of June. The Arabs' only saviours were alcohol, hashish and the haunting strains of Um Kalthum. Everything else was lost.

How often I thought of taking my own life!

I looked everywhere for a gun, but I could not get hold of one. There were some firearms that I knew of, but they were all kept under lock and key at the party headquarters, and I could never bring myself to ask for one. Even death was only obtainable after getting official approval and written permission in triplicate from the correct authorities! In life and death we were governed by people who build castles in the air and who yawn with the boredom of the days.

1967. After the war.

The morning session of the Conference of Resistance came to an end and we left the assembly hall with our heads like empty boxes now filled with all the rubbish that had been spoken inside. We could have gone on speechifying and reciting poems until defeat had been turned into victory.

I bombard my friends with questions, and they reply with questions of their own. I try to find a moment of security in embraces with the men among them. Each of us is trembling with fear and cold. Each of us imagines the endless waves of fighter-bombers dropping their load of explosives and contempt down on our bodies. I feel like an old woman, bereft of support, holding up a lamp to the darkness in the search for her lost youth. I could not bring myself to recite my poetry. I could not bring myself to listen to the poetry of others. Most of the time I was with other writers, and we had to be careful not to let our eyes meet. I thought perhaps we could go back into ourselves one day and look for the primitive apes which are within us. I dragged myself to my room at the hotel and tried to sleep in order to forget the pantomime. But sleep does not come easily and the heat of Cairo burns my solitude. The walls of my room seem to be closing in on me. The map of the Arab world looks like a prison. I hear the chains and shackles being put around me. But when I explore my body I find I am still alive.

The phone rings. I ignore it. It will only be one of them. One of those idiots who made me sick during the morning, with their talk about the masses and the great battle ahead. The phone does not stop ringing. Realizing that the person on the other end is not going to give up, I lift the receiver, putting a stop to the hollowness of hesitation, and I hear a man's voice. I do not recognise it at first:

"You weren't asleep were you? What about the afternoon session?"

I feel like telling him what he can do with his afternoon session. We play the role of audience, plays and the stage itself. To hell with their conference and their speeches and their celebrations.

The voice went on:

"It's Issam Hatim here. I wanted to have a word with you about something. And don't worry, it hasn't got anything to do with the conference."

Issam Hatim. I remember him from my time at University. His thin frame, his pained expression, his eyes which used to have a far-away look in them as though he had fallen out of the sky and was still looking for his star up there in the night. We used to talk about the need for change in the Arab world. Most of all I remember his being a dedicated Palestinian who was willing to give up everything for the cause. I remember the miserable days when we were in Arum. Issam would come to us in the café over the road from the Military Museum, carrying his papers and his poems. He would read us his latest *qasida* and then look around at our faces to see what we thought.

Sometimes we would fall out over our differences. We both belonged to progressive parties, but while my party operated out in the open, his believed in covert action. His face on the night of the Fifth of June, with the knives of defeat raining down upon us relentlessly; it wore a look which I shall never forget.

I tell him that I will be right down. Why am I so keen to see him? Is it pleasure in seeing someone even worse off than myself that drives me on, or the chance to wound or to settle old scores? These thoughts evaporate as I go down the stairs. What desire to wound? Who is right and who is wrong, anyway? Neither his party nor mine, neither their politicians nor ours could do a thing to put right what had happened.

We embrace like old friends, and we talk about the past for a few moments, before jumping back to the present. I ask him how life has been treating him since we left the classroom. His hollow eyes sparkle and without any preliminaries he asks me:

"Are you still in the party?"

I smile bitterly.

"I left it. Or rather, I was distanced from it. My comrades found that I was unsuitable for the struggle. Bullets and poems are not good partners it seems." Then I add: "I was just a petite-bourgeoise intellectual in a revolutionary party."

We smile at each other and look in one another's faces for the marks which time has left there. The passage of time leaves traces on everything. I ask Issam:

"What about you?"

"I left as well. It seems that there are hardly any differences between the political parties any more."

"You were at the conference, weren't you?"

He saw the irony of my words.

"You haven't changed a bit. Just the same as always. Yes, I went to some of the sessions."

"Did you recite any of your poetry?"

"Oh, I delivered a few rousing odes!"

"Aren't they ashamed of themselves? Imagine! Yusuf still insists on banging on with his grand words."

"Why should they be ashamed of themselves? Impertinence is everywhere."

The silence engulfs us. Oh, for those moments when we return to the depths of ourselves after a long absence and see ourselves as we really are. I look at his face, and at my own face when, long ago, I used to talk about victory, when I still felt able to recite my poetry and repeat slogans, when I still believed in what I was taught at school.

I say to him:

"What are you doing these days? It's been a while since we met. Have you left Arum."

"Left Arum? You know that I couldn't ever do that . . . At the moment some comrades and I are setting up an armed Palestinian resistance organization. It's our conviction that the only way to turn around all these losses is with the gun."

I was hearing a new voice speaking to me over the symphony of defeat, a voice coming from tomorrow, a voice of repudiation and rejection, a voice which transcended our surrender and our never-ending failures. They had picked up guns, but not to commit suicide, as I had wanted to do: they were going to fight back.

We carried on talking for a long time and we discussed many things. We talked about the theoretical paths which had led us to where we were. We talked about our major concerns at that stage and the possibility of laying down alternatives to the existing political structures standing over the Arab world.

And he asked me if I would like to join their organization.

My body trembles. Should I agree? What else could I do? I couldn't keep on writing poetry, reciting it to assemblies of bored men trying to get away from their wives, having women repeating it to their lovers. My audiences all end up talking about something else anyway: the weather and what the neighbours have been getting up to. What alternative did I have?

I say to Issam:

"I'll join. Do you have a place for me?"

"There's a place for everyone."

The following day I leave Cairo bound for Arum. I go to my boss at the newspaper where I work and throw my resignation in his face. For a moment he looks at me like an idiot and then has the nerve to ask me out to dinner that night. I walk out, leaving behind me my co-workers all dreaming of how much they will get in their next pay rise, leaving the piles of words which they will continue to churn out. I leave my old face behind, the face disfigured by war. I go out into the streets of Arum feeling like a new woman. I am free of the submission which is built into my humanity, free of my own weakness, free of the myth of mourning which had become ingrained in my blood.

Free.

I head for the town by the sea, where my parents are waiting. I tell my father of my plans. He gets angry and goes around the house, shouting and breaking things. Finally he falls helplessly into his chair. I do not move. I stare at the floor and keep silent.

"What if you are killed?"

"Don't worry. I'll come back."

I go to my room and begin to gather a few things together. When he has regained some of his composure, he follows me to my room.

"And what if you don't come back?"

"Then my life will have ended just as if it had ended in some stupid, meaningless car accident."

At least he had the decency not to mention family honour and my virginity this time.

He doesn't say a word, but looks at me without expression. Then he goes out and closes the door. I confront the silence. It is broken only by my mother's voice raised in prayer at the other end of the big house. For a long time now she had not left her bed. She just lies there, writing me letters, praying for me, mourning the loss of the rich husband who slipped through my fingers. I kiss her goodbye, without telling her about my trip, and I leave her to her prayers.

I take my leave of the town and the sea and the jujube trees. I look at the faces of people as if I am seeing them for the first time. The faces which are familiar to me fade away as the car moves in the direction of Arum. I reach there just before dawn. The humidity of September envelops the trees and the pavements and the windows of the coffee-houses. I head towards my house and find it drenched in tedium, in dresses, in perfume. I open the clothes cupboard and take out a few things for my journey. I put them in a small hold-all and I think to myself that this is the first time I have left home without taking my perfume and my poetry with me . . . without my papers and my camera. I shall go and encounter the earth. I shall meet the men who have found a way that leads to Jerusalem.

I arrive in Harran. Issam meets me at the door of the headquarters. He holds out his arms and I throw myself into his embrace. War has brought us together again. He accompanies me to the house of Um Abed, one of the women members of the Organization. She was in her fifties and you might say that she was the consummate woman of the Palestinian revolution. Whenever I think of her now, her memory inspires the tenderest of feelings in my heart. The Organization would use her to spread word of the struggle among the people in the refugee camps around Harran, as well as in other towns. She would move through the streets carrying our important documents and our publications, and then she would come back in the evening with medicine, clothes and money. Um Abed was braver than bravery itself. Many of the members of our women's organization would refuse to accompany her on the missions she undertook. She showed me the meaning of perseverance and taught me to speak plainly. She also told me about the history of the Palestinian exodus which brought them here to the groves of exile.

"I can't sleep, Um Abed. I am filled with anxiety."

"You must sleep, Nadia. Tomorrow is going to be a tiring day."

I try to fall asleep but I can't – sleep cheated me during my nights in Harran – so I hug my pillow and ask Um Abed to tell me about her life for a while.

"Jerusalem was surrounded and it fell into enemy hands. I was on a visit to my aunt near the al-Aqsa Mosque. We heard that the last section of the city had now come under enemy occupation which meant that I couldn't get back to my family any more for seven years. I didn't know what had happened to them, until one day I was listening to the radio and I heard my mother reading out a message to the members of her family who were under enemy occupation. She said that all my brothers and sisters had got away safely. At the end of the message she broke down in tears and the announcer finished off the message for her in the traditional way, saying "Be comforted and give comfort to others."

"What made you join this organization? Are you a Marxist?"

Without knowing it, this simple woman could sum up the whole of Marxist ideology to me in two sentences:

"The rich fight because they want to hang onto their possessions. The poor fight because they have nothing to lose. I chose this group because they speak on behalf of the poor."

Um Abed had no idea about the world of politics. She appeared among us as one who was living an adventure which pleased her. She was completely convinced of the rectitude of Palestinian resistance and if the ways and means of the various groups were different, in the end they all shared the same aim, to liberate our land.

"They're all Palestinians, Nadia. They all share the same goal."

It was to Um Abed with her pure heart that I turned with all my worries and problems and she taught me how to bear everything with fortitude. I would come to her after a long day in the camps, and she would do all she could to help me relax and to prepare the ideological leaflets which we issued. I would complain to her about the crises which we faced and she would open up new horizons for me. There was one night when our comrades were surrounded by another armed Palestinian Fedeyeen group at Beit Ibrahim. There had been a quarrel at one of the bases. I came running over to Um Abed to tell her the news. She picked up a pistol and went out to Beit Ibrahim alone. I followed her and grabbed her by the arm.

"Um Abed, you can't go by yourself. There are at least fifteen of them and they're armed."

She took no notice of my entreaties and continued on her way. Within half an hour she had returned. The two parties had been separated without a single shot being fired.

The day I was parted from Um Abed was one of the saddest days of my life. I was to go up to one of the military encampments in the North. I was in great pain when I finally said goodbye to her. She waved and then was lost in the gloom. The only time I ever saw her again was when she came to me at the house where they kept me after the Geneva operation. She kissed me on both cheeks and handed me a bag of za'tar, the special Palestinian thyme which she knew I was very fond of. When I got back to Ayntab I found out that Um Abed had been killed in action that September. Her body had been found at the door of the Organization offices. It was riddled with bullets. I do not know where they buried her, but every time I think of her in my loneliness, I wish that I were lying at her side.

Midnight. Fifth of September 1977.

I am still here, glued to my seat in this café, thinking about a face in a far-off land. The night of exile. Your chest which embraces the shattered remnants of my body. The remains of defeat and sorrow. You. The man in whose body I tried to forget my past, but who made it flare up inside me. The man in whose eyes I tried to find a homeland to which I could flee, but who sent me back to my homeland instead. Frank. Exile. This exile that we share together. You and I are a past which is still alive, alive in our heads. You and I are the screams of our comrades contained by prison walls and tombs. We spend our days talking about a way of forgetting their eyes at the moment that they were forcibly taken from us.

The day when we first met?

Oh yes, I remember that. The lecture hall filled with students from Third World countries. You talking about Palestine, Central America and Africa. I have come to listen to you. I have come to see you, now that you are out of prison and back in the land of milk and honey. My friend tells me that you have finally given in to your bourgeois background and that you are content with the memory of your former comrades. You have come back to France to write stories about them and how they met their deaths. The beautiful scented ladies received you as a hero, and your name is proclaimed from their temples.

They needed a myth, so they fashioned one out of your life and gave it to a country which no longer has any legends of its own. You became a star. They put you on a pedestal like an idol to worship.

Expert on revolution. Consultant on the affairs of 'the Dark Continent' . . . which now lies in flames.

What they did not know was that they were actually killing you, that they were pushing you into an obscure corner where memory and oblivion could rot together.

I level my gaze at you. In the middle of your analysis of the inconsistencies of revolution in the Arab states, I interrupt you and say:

"Don't talk about Palestine until you know what you are talking about."

You are stung by my words. You want to say something but the words die as you try to speak them. Our eyes met as if in a mirror. You follow me to a café next to the University.

"Who are you?"

I do not reply, but you don't give up. I can see the determination in your eyes. It is the determination of a man who is dying of pain. I give you a little smile and say:

"I see you are trying with all your strength to forget about your past."

"The past has gone. It is all over. Now I am here in France, where I was born. I write so that I can live with myself. I have children so that I can live through them. Here I can struggle against the reactionary elements of my class."

I remain silent. I know all about your dilemma between allegiance to your former comrades and the temptation to return to your bourgeois roots. But I also know that you have already made your decision. I know that you have chosen ease and resignation. I know that you live between your three houses. I know how hard you find it to smile these days.

"You are playing right into the hands of the bourgeoisie. You'll end up as Minister of Culture if you're not careful!"

"Only when the Left wins in France. I didn't betray my comrades. You just have to remember that every country is different."

I say nothing. Why do I accuse you? Why do I impale you on the blade of my own doubt and weakness? I, too, have turned into a fortress withstanding the onslaught of past memories. I, too, am looking for excuses for my escape, and am seeking to justify my life here, far away from Ayntab.

Frank! Why am I remembering all this. The night is nearly over, Frank, and the wind is beating on the city. Here I am, sitting at a corner table in a Parisian café, waiting for some kind of redemption. I can see the face of Um Abed in the reflection of the café windows. I can hear her voice as I was leaving Harran to go to the training camps.

"Nadia, you are the first of the women guerrillas. It is vital that you don't throw your life away."

Well, I did not throw my life away. I survived to roam the pavements of exile. But my life was taken away. In much the same way, you survived and your mentor died in the jungle. We are two sides of the same coin. How irksome this silence between us is. How banal are the days in which we live.

One day I say to Issam:

"I want to take military training. I want to do active service."

The military council meets to take its decision on my joining up with one of the military bases. Their discussion takes a long time. How could a woman possibly live among fighting-men? However, I was adamant, and in the end they gave in: "Her experience will be a good way of encouraging other women to take up our cause. Why shouldn't we give it a try?"

That is how Issam wound up the discussion which sent me off to a new life. I moved to a world of canvas and weapons. All the wrangling and petty arguing that went on between the political parties was behind me now, along with all the old comrades who were still rotting in jail cells, with no one in their respective parties prepared to make a stand that would actually bring them back into an effective sphere of the struggle. Every night I read your books and I light up my soul with the words you have written. I read things by al-Munsif, your comrade too. I look again at the history of revolutions and the men who made that history. Vietnam. Cuba. Bolivia. In their footsteps we look for guidance in our own struggle. I tell my comrades how our struggle is special and how the difficulties that we are facing have not been encountered by any other revolutionary group. The sound of our voices sees in the new day, and daylight passes with the search for our roots which tie us to the earth.

Today is the Fifth of September and where is the struggle now? Has it been stifled?

Ayntab is not the end of the world and there is enough room in historical memory to encompass other towns and other martyrs and refugees. I breathe in the warmth of the café and I listen to the voices of the drinkers. I think about going to one of my friends for help and sharing something of the torment which I am going through. Maybe that way I can stop it galloping through the carefully guarded vaults of calm and surrender within me.

But my friends have all left Paris. Where is al-Bahi, who could bury me according to his own special ceremony? Where is Muhammad, the Ambassador of Hate, who rails against all things? Where are the Sa'alik? Why can't they all come to me now and release me from memory and help me to forget the face of him who has gone away.

The commander of the military camp was not able hide his surprise when he first saw me:

"You're here at last . . . But, when I heard you were coming, I expected you to be . . . I mean, what makes a young and beautiful girl like you chose a life of danger?"

This makes me laugh. I answer all his questions. He asks me whether I would like to start organizing our work.

On the southern borders of an Arab country near to the field of battle, our camp consists of a group of fighters whose faces were coloured by the sun. They wait for each night with joy in their hearts. Their talk is of liberation and martyrdom. We would meet and talk in small groups. Farhan would tell us stories about his days in the refugee camps. Sa'id would make us all laugh with his silly jokes. We would listen to recitations of the poems of Mahmoud Darwish and Samih al-Qasim. We would re-read the memoirs of Che Guevara on the eve of the famous blockade. After midnight, when the stars were in the last portion of the sky, the group would pick up their arms and spread out over the plains. We monitored the enemy's movements on the other side of the border, keeping away from the lights. It was cold and we had to blow on our hands to keep them warm. The first days were difficult. The sun was our enemy. I search for dreams of revolution. I search for the colourful images of guerrilla fighters that used to fire my imagination: men who did not need to eat or sleep, men who shunned the love of women, men who could leap high walls and land on the other side unscathed. But those I meet are all ordinary men who laugh, and eat, and who sometimes are afraid. I try to reconcile the differences between what I dreamt and what I saw.

I begin weapons training for real. I hold a rifle in my hand for the first time. I become familiar with the different kinds of weapons and telescopic sights, including an old French service rifle which had a kick on it that I can still feel to this day. I liked the Czech rifles most of all. In the first two months after my arrival I used everything from small pistols to heavy machine guns, including M-16s, Thompsons, Carlos and Kalashnikov Ak-47s.

Three months go by. Four months. I can hardly stand it any more. I no longer have the patience required for this seemingly endless training. What's more, they seem not to have confidence in me. I am a woman and I do not really speak the same language as them. I talk about ideology their preferred topic of conversation is the towns in the Arab world where they have lived, and their grasp of ideological discourse is almost non-existent. I see it as my job to do something about their political naïvety. What I need to do is to find a way of closing the linguistic gap which is keeping us apart. That is the hardest thing as far as I am concerned. Che Guevara comes to mind during the moments that I am alone and unoccupied. It is he who makes me remember that I must find the bridges that link them and me. I stare at the face of Che Guevara which accompanies me wherever I go. My comrades look like heroes as they wait in the early hours of the morning for the moment of action.

Some days pass quickly. Others seem to drag on forever. The camp commandant is replaced by a new fighter. His name is Abu Mashour and he is younger than most of us and his awesome courage is displayed as we get to know each other during the course of time. He has devoted his whole life to the Palestinian cause and Palestine has taken complete possession of his being. To me he is the perfect man. Today, when I am frightened by the unlit streets and the cold rooms in the frozen continent of Europe, or when I see people giving up on their revolutionary ideals, I think bitterly of Abu Mashour. He gave me many a lesson in organization and taught me how to obey orders without uttering a single word of dissent.

Abu Mashour talks to me about al-Teera, the village where he was born. And where is al-Teera?

"Where do you think, Nadia! It's where Palestine is. It could only be in Palestine. That's where the old man passed away."

The old man?

"My father. When he died, only three people could make it to the funeral: the Shaykh of the mosque, my brother and the grave digger. They buried him with the explosions of 1948 ringing in their ears. And he left us in this world."

At other times we talk about the life in the camps and the role of the United Nations Relief and Works Agency. Who do they suppose they are relieving? The world of flesh and blood was silent. Abu Mashour was silent. The waves of brown ether awaken in those hours of the night of the southern plains of one of the Arab countries. Midnight strikes. I am filled with joy at being one of them. I love Abu Mashour's stories. I feel there is a mysterious ring in them, like a stifled lament, a hidden intonation which causes the syllables to disintegrate. The clock strikes. We go back to the camp. Death stares at us from the other side. Our weapons are in our hands and we wait.

The days I spend under the sun and the nights I spend listening to the stories of Abu Mashour. I become emancipated in my own destiny as a woman. I become like a tree, a sacred woman-tree, my branches growing outwards as I take control of my own body and soul. I am a woman who holds her own death in her hands. The myth of summer ends and night begins to creep along the paths like a sharp wind blowing through our bones. When shall we enter the field of battle? Abu Mashour laughs:

"You look like you are ready to jump out of your skin, Nadia. Don't worry. The time is coming and the battle will be long."

We throw bundles of wild foliage under our bodies and we embrace the earth. We smell the rain and what the days ahead hold in store for us. The city is nothing but a dim and distant memory. For months we have not breathed the city air, nor have we smelt our bodies in the luxurious comfort of urban life. We resist and we revolt against temptation, blocking it out of our minds, keeping it from swaying our will. But far be it for us to change the sophisticated world of urban existence. We keep our faces and our expressions to ourselves. Only our smiles show how much our bodies are yearning and the smiles go quickly in the memory of the moment.

One day Issam arrives at the camp. He takes me to one side and tells me that my life is about to change. I ask him what he means by that. He tells me to prepare myself to leave immediately. I go and get my things. In the struggle, even the slightest hesitation or lack of co-operation is not tolerated. I look at the face of Abu Mashour as we sit side by side in the jeep on our way to the South. The camp lies behind us with its simple lights burning like the fires of expectation. I whisper into my comrade's ear to ask him if he knows where we are heading. He shakes his head. Issam remains silent. The driver smokes his cigarette calmly. The winds of the southern plains flow into our bodies and we shiver with the cold. The jeep continues on its way and no one says a word. We reach the border of Harran. We are stopped at a checkpoint. With an air of boredom – "More guerrilla fighters going to and fro!" – the officer in charge asks to see our ID cards. He looks them over and sniffs contemptuously, saying that he wants to see our real ID's next time. Abu Mashour smiles. I smile. What can he mean? Those are the only ID's we have. In fact we have come to the only real stage of our lives. Before this we had nothing. No identity papers. No reality. We continue on our way towards the south. We leave the main road, and sail through olive groves and holm forests. The jeep stops and the three of us get out. We are close to a hill over which we can see a halo of lights coming from a military encampment behind. Issam goes ahead of us. His long strides seem to be part of the night. We follow him. A voice in the distance asks for the password. I hear Issam reply: "Geneva."

The word surprises me. I thought he might be pulling our legs, just like he used to do in days of the café over the road from the military museum. We pass inside a small tent which is lit by a gas lamp. We come face to face with two men who were inside the tent waiting for us. Issam introduces us: Saleh and Farhan, Nadia and Abu Mashour. These are faces which have been with me many times in operations that I have carried out since that meeting. We settle down on the earth inside the tent and there is silence for a moment. It had to be something important for an emergency meeting to be called like this. Issam spoke first:

"Comrade Nadia used to be in charge of publicity at the Husaini camp. She's a revolutionary poet and speaks English fluently.

"Comrade Abu Mashour is one of our best fighters. He's been trained in urban guerrilla warfare in Cuba.

"Comrade Saleh used to be an army officer in another of the Arab countries. He flies Mig XVII fighters.

"Comrade Farhan is an explosives expert. He used to be a chemical scientist."

We look around at each other's faces, trying to see further than the information that we have just been given. Then we look at Issam and wait for him to tell us the circumstances which have brought us to this place.

"Central command has decided to broaden the scope of our struggle. It is our intention to make sure the whole world knows about the Palestinian cause and we will show them that we are here fighting for the return of our land."

The silence which followed was like a nocturnal bird coming to rest upon us. The others were clearly in the same position as me as far as not being informed about the reason for this sudden gathering. Issam paused for a moment and then began speaking again.

"Central command has been looking at the feasibility of our carrying out operations externally, outside the Arab arena."

"What do you mean exactly?" I interrupted.

"America and Western Europe."

My mind is immediately filled with thoughts about the bloody attacks made by various Latin American revolutionary groups in Europe . . . the settling of old scores . . . the struggle western intelligence services had in dealing with the last vestiges of Nazism . . . the hunt for Trotsky which ended with his assassination. I was afraid that my comrades were going to trigger off a chain of events which might lead to a similar conclusion.

"What kind of operations do you have in mind?"

"Hijacking airliners, planting bombs on the premises of companies which supply arms to Israel, targeting American companies in the Middle East."

No one moved or spoke. The seconds passed slowly. All eyes were turned on me, waiting for me to take the initiative. My mind was racing. To me the idea seemed like madness in view of the fact that the struggle was not even properly established in the Arab theatre. Up until then, our organization could barely muster enough support to carry out operations in the Occupied Land itself.

Abu Mashour asks Issam:

"What are the strategic goals of operations like these?"

"To tell the world that we are here. We all know that reactionary governments can do away with us any time it suits them to do so. Furthermore, it is our intention to stop this current wave of colonization which is occurring in the Occupied Land."

Abu Mashour's face is filled with doubt and questions.

"I don't think you are going about this in the right way, comrade. The struggle must have its feet placed firmly here in the Arab arena. You can't win the battle with publicity."

Issam asks me my opinion. He waits. I hesitate a moment so that the woman-tree can stretch out her branches and free herself from her fear and her mortality.

"There is nothing wrong with extending the scope of our struggle in this way, but external operations must be backed up by action in the Occupied Land itself. That said, I have never been against external operations."

The discussion goes on until morning and we finish up accepting the decision of the military command. We are to go to Geneva to carry out the first operation there.

Abu Mashour's face is filled with despondency. His eyes move to the gas lamp and he stares at the flickering yellow flame. He takes up a twig in his hand, and then, like a highly-strung colt, he begins to scratch the ground in front of him.

The orders are clear. The night's discussion determines that we are to change the mode of our lives and the style of our training. We move to a special camp and begin an onerous course of training in urban guerrilla tactics. The first hours of the day we spend doing close target practice. We concentrate on using our reflex capabilities. We start memorising the map of Europe: its airports, its cities, the climatic conditions, everything. In the evening, I return to my tent and brush up on my English.

A few days into training, and I have reached proficiency in firing at long and short distances. My comrades were surprised by my fast progress, after they had seen the initial difficulty I had in handling the weapons. That's how I am, though. I tend to reject everything that is new, but after a while I always get the hang of it.

Do you remember, Frank.

Once, I found a 6 mm revolver in a drawer at your place. I picked it up and checked the safety catch. I put it back and turned around to find that you had been watching me in silence. You had seen the way my hands had moved around the weapon and there was a look of strange curiosity on your face. I knew that there was the germ of an idea in your head at that moment. I smiled as I said to you:

"You know, I'm scared by the sight of weapons."

Without smiling back, you said:

"That's not the impression I got. I could tell by the way you picked up that revolver that you have been properly trained in how to use it."

I did not make any comment on what you had said. I was afraid of suddenly throwing away my false papers and producing my real passport, the one which gives my mother's and father's real names, and to seek refuge in the Nadia whom I used to be. It is not easy for a fighter to hide his or her real identity from another fighter. We bow to the same set of rules. Those rules follow us wherever we go, in the way we talk and the way we think, even in the way we move.

Yes, Frank. I know how to use a gun. I learnt under the hot sun of the East at a camp which has been wiped off the face of this earth.

They told me there that my gun was my most precious possession. If I lost it, I would lose my life.

They told me there the pistol is the most important of all the different types of weapons used in urban warfare: it's light and can be easily concealed.

I told them how much I hated the thought of killing someone in the cold light of day. I can't stand to see death or to live by it. War out in the open, in the desert or in the fields, is much more humane and bearable. In the urban environment, you stand face to face with your enemy. There are those that are frightened and those who play God. We fire off rounds at a range of between one and three metres, and the principle is very simple: you either kill or you get killed. Out in the open, you get a good chance of not having to stare death in the face, one way or the other.

Back in the camp. October and November are like terrifying *jinn*. The rains wash the oaktrees. Winter has begun and the operation will start in a matter of days. Abu Mashour and I spend a lot of time together. At six in the morning we wake up and do our exercises. We do route marches. We mow the grass around the entrances to the camp. We strip down and reassemble our weapons. All the time we are doing these things, he and I talk about many different subjects.

He tells me he does not believe that the operation we are about to undertake will serve any useful purpose. I reply by telling him:

"You must think beyond that. We have to get publicity for our cause."

He goes on to tell me about his father, and how he was gunned down before his eyes in the village of al-Teera. He tells me about his brother who lost an eye in 1948, and about the days he spent in the refugee camps. I, on the other hand, had little to tell him. My father was still alive. What did I know about homelessness or life in the camps? My childhood resounded with long speeches about my blue blood. Yellow blood. Red blood.

If I had told Abu Mashour about my father's speeches he would have found it hilarious and made fun of me for months afterwards. If I had breathed a word about my rich suitor whose departure had caused my mother so much grief, Abu Mashour would have probably thought it the funniest thing he'd ever heard and from then on he would have called me something like 'Fortune's widow.' I did not say a word about my past life. Anyway, I thought he probably suspected what kind of life I had led.

We talk a lot about the land. We talk a lot about the past. We talk a lot about the present and the future. It is hard for a Palestinian to talk about land without talking about the past as well. In the same way, he is scarcely able to talk about the future without his land. One evening, Abu Mashour comes to me with a copy of Regis Debray's *Revolution in the Revolution*. We spend the whole night reading it together, stopping at places where Debray defines the duty of revolutionary focus. I disagree with his making Cuba the basis for his observations. It is hard to extrapolate generalizations from what was a unique event.

Abu Mashour takes up my point, his eyes gleaming in the darkness.

"Debray's mistake is that he gives too much prominence to the intellectual élite. I agree with him over the minor role of the decadent political parties, but I think he gives too little significance to the role played by those in alliance with the intellectual élite.

"I suppose he thought that way because he was one of the intelligentsia himself. He found it difficult to get along with the revolutionaries and they spurned him for a long time."

I remain silent for a moment. I am reminded of the sterile debates which used to go on in university and at the writers' union. I say to my friend:

"You know that I don't particularly trust the intellectual élite either, but it is hard for me to understand the language of the down-to-earth fighting men. That is something that I've found out here in the camp. Before, I used to dream about living this kind of life while I was at university and at the writers' union. Back then I hated anyone like me. I couldn't stand my peers. I couldn't stand the aura of smug satisfaction which hung around them, the lack of awareness, the disbelief in the absolute power of imagination. The moment I joined this group, and took up the struggle with them, I discovered what it meant to have an appetite for life."

"When you lose touch with your roots it's hard to put down new roots in a different piece of ground. You'll always be an outsider. We are a different kind of person altogether. We have our good points and our bad points. Our worst characteristic is our lack of interest in things which do not directly serve the cause and which do not play a part in the struggle. Therefore, because things like music, sex, gazing into the eyes of a lover, the smell of jasmine, dreams, because none of these have any bearing on the struggle, we become strangers to them and to ourselves, and it is not something that we can ever change."

Abu Mashour has put his finger on the wound.

"But you are my brothers and you always will be. I have no family other than you. I have become used to your daily routine and I have stood up to everything that has been thrown at me. The pain is bearable because of the laughter, and laughter like this is not possible without faith in something out there beyond life and the transience of the moment."

The night seeps into our blood. The wind whistles over the southern plains of that Arab country which lies to the north of its neighbours. The wind whistles and the night is reaching its last hours. We are two oaks at the edge of the forest, waiting for the sun and the rain and the wind. While we wait, we stretch out our branches and embrace. Our faces come close together. I say to him:

"Tomorrow we go to Geneva. Are you prepared?"

"What do you mean? I trained as much as you did."

"That's not what I meant. What I'm talking about is whether you believe that the operation will do any good. You were opposed to the idea at first."

"Well, I'm still not certain what the outcome will be. All I know is that I will carry out the orders issued by the military command, even if I know that some of their orders are ill-advised and that the leaders sometimes make mistakes. I'll never forget that they have their history and background and I have mine, and you will never get the two to coincide."

The night slips silently into our blood and the daylight starts to show in the Eastern skies behind the hill. The night draws itself from my body and the body of the darkness. I look around at the camp and the face of my comrade. Whatever was going to happen in the coming days, I was no longer afraid of dying. It had ceased to matter the moment I discovered that it wasn't important for me to be the link between my father and the future generation. The jeep arrives and we get in. There are no personal belongings for someone who is fighting for a cause. Sometimes, there isn't even love.

Frank!

It is the last part of the night. I am still stuck to my seat in the corner of a café. On my body are the traces of the wind and the bitter cold of this terrible town. You are in my head. The faces of all my comrades. The fires raging in Ayntab. How much I need your hands, your eyes, your chest. How much I need you, with the remnants of your revolt, prison, your struggle against memory. But since yesterday, I have lost my ability to forget. The woman-tree has been re-awakened and the danger has passed. I must stand up. I must resist.

Snow covers the face of Geneva. Through the window of the plane it looks totally white, featureless. The plane approaches the runway.

I remember the moment we arrived at Geneva Airport. The first time my feet were placed on this ancient and icy continent of Europe. At my side, the face of Abu Mashour. His eyes, as I had become used to them by that time, full of unanswered questions. His questions seemed to be like long sentences stretching through time.

We move through the brightly lit corridors towards the police barriers. We hand over our US Passports and wait. A few minutes later we are in the Customs Hall. Things are over quickly and we have little trouble getting into Switzerland. We can now unburden ourselves of the fear and hesitation which we have been carrying with us. We are on the verge of freedom. After a short while we will have it in our grasp.

According to the information which I received, we were to go to the Ritz Hotel, at 23, Danfire Rocheroi Street. On arrival there, I was to contact another comrade who was coming from Germany. It was to be his job to take care of things during our stay in Geneva.

We are soon out of the airport buildings. We hardly look at the faces of the people walking past us. I have none of the usual feelings of pleasure about arriving in a new city. New cities used to mean release and lack of restraint to me, new discoveries and adventures, but in Geneva I found myself counting and recounting the seconds. Abu Mashour lent over to me and whispered in my ear:

"Don't forget that we're meant to be married. You've got to play your part properly."

I smile. Spots of light rain bathe my hair. We get into one of the taxis waiting at the airport. The driver takes us to the address that we have been given. The Ritz Hotel stands next to Lake Léman on the west side of Geneva, halfway between the monument to the Unknown Soldier and the Lausanne Road. It overlooks the lake, which was frozen in the harsh Swiss winter.

The car stops in front of the hotel. The driver speaks to us in French, but his accent is either German or Italian . . . it could have been Maltese, for all I knew.

"Here's your hotel. I'll stop for a moment and help you get your luggage out."

I leave Abu Mashour to help the driver and I go through to the hotel lobby. The warmth of the hotel hits me. It gives me a sense of security. The time is about eight-thirty and our appointment with the comrade from Germany is set for nine o'clock. That gives me just half an hour to wash, change clothes, and get some rest. I wait for Abu

Mashour to come to the reception. We approach the clerk and ask for the key to the room that was booked for us. He hands it over, along with an envelope which he tells us was left for us just under an hour ago.

We go to the lift. Another hotel employee follows us, carrying our bags. He does not stop talking. He has probably been talking ever since the lake gave in to the onslaught of the icy wind, and Geneva's nights lived longer than her days.

"Oh, there's been such a lot of snow this winter. What a pity that you're here when it's so cold. It'll be so much nicer when the spring comes. The lake's been frozen for days. All the wild ducks have flown away. But they'll be back again soon along with all the pigeons."

He is muttering away in French and I try to give him the impression that I am taking part in the conversation. We get to the fifth floor, where our room is situated. We go down the long corridor and arrive at the room. It is a beautiful and spacious room with a window overlooking the lake and a view of the Swiss Alps on the other side, stretching away towards the plains of France. The hotel employee shows us the telephone, the bathroom, the lavatory and the buzzer which calls room service, everything.

Finally he goes out. I open the envelope which I got with the keys and take out its contents. It is a message from our comrade from Germany telling us that he would not be able to meet us at nine o'clock.

I feel a pang of anxiety which I try to hide from Abu Mashour. I ask myself whether something has happened which might affect our plans. I go to the bathroom and try to wash from my face the traces of the tiring journey which we have made from Ayntab to Geneva. The telephone rings and I run over to it. It is the comrade from Germany. He tells me that he can now make it after all at nine-thirty. We get dressed. No words are exchanged between us. We set out for the restaurant which lies no more than three hundred metres away from the hotel. It was an Italian restaurant, I think, and it was lit by candles that evening. For some reason the Swiss love candlelight and, on every possible occasion, they dispense with electricity and light candles instead. We speak to one another in English. The other comrade begins by telling us that the date for the operation has had to be brought forward by a day or two. One of the British airlines was on strike which meant that El-Al were making more journeys to the Middle East than usual.

The comrade stares right at me. Two sunburned faces staring at each other, two young people, neither of them more than twenty-five years old. Borders and towns and men's faces are disappearing before my eyes. I have this great desire for the hours to become minutes, for time to be shortened and for the job to be finished as quickly as possible. I remember Issam's face, his voice right out of the Palestinian refugee camps, his hollow eyes:

"We have been surrounded and it won't be long before they come and finish us off. We've got to get the message to our people in the camps so that they can keep the enemy at bay just a little longer."

I remember the Fifth of June. Defeat. Failure. Speeches. The party which I belonged to. The party which brought me up and which filled my head with those sterile, barren notions: theoretical struggle, the proletariat, justice.

I remember the day I left them. I was exhausted by my pain and disappointment, so I took flight, like a bird in autumn. The party secretary said to me: "I'm sorry to see you go, Nadia. I thought that we could make something of you in this party. But I see now that I was wrong."

I replied with fire burning in my head and my blood and my nerves:

"I was just an ignorant docile little pet among you, wasn't I? You lot would need to come out of your mothers' wombs again before you could see the reality which the war has brought about. The struggle is now a nationalist one, and our enemy is doing its best to wipe us off the face of this earth. We have got to arm ourselves and fight back."

I remember that he came up with an argument from Lenin's 'lessons from the Moscow movement of 1916' which said that you should never resort to arms.

But I told him that Lenin also said in that same publication that you should rely on force in a more serious and vital manner within a framework of greater zeal. You have to explain to the masses the futility of general strikes and the like, and that violent and extreme measures must necessarily be a direct goal of the struggle in the future.

"If you ignore that part of what Lenin was saying, you are deceiving yourselves," I said to him: "Read the book again, comrade, and I'd make sure you read it properly this time. The time has come for us to really speak our minds."

I look into the faces of my comrades. Two Palestinian faces, the faces of two members of the people who realised quickly the solution to their problems was the gun. They realised it a few days after the fall of the phoney masks of the political parties, whose days were spent in books, and waiting for the sound of the bells to come from afar to define for them the purpose of their movements.

The woman inside me is awakened. The woman wakes up as a girl who shivers in the cold of the nights which are so unlike the warmth of the Mediterranean and the hearts of the mountains close by. I remember the Mediterranean in front of me, and my father. . . .

Suddenly I notice that my two comrades are staring at me and they start laughing.

"Where were you, Nadia? You were miles away just then."

"I was thinking how much need there is for revolution in the countries that we have just left behind us."

"What else is new!" said Abu Mashour, and he carried on his conversation with the other comrade.

I think of you. My head is lit up with thoughts of you. I was addicted to reading your books as well as those of your mentor. I tried to find out about my own reality in the light of your experiences in the jungles of those far-off lands. How did you manage to escape to the icy towns of Europe? I think about the snowy night, and the lights around the lakes.

The restaurant is filled with beautiful women. Warmth exudes from everything. Doubt has turned into certainty in my mind about the benefit of the operation my comrades and I are about to undertake. Why shouldn't their ease be shaken up a bit, when they've given themselves over to such opulence? Why not indeed? Just a little shock to their systems. Let it rain blood down onto their clean streets for a while. Let them see that there are people out there who have nothing to eat and nowhere to live. Everything I see seems to be telling me to get on with the job. And where should we do it? It didn't really matter.

That night in Geneva was the last night for a man and woman who had come in search of their identity, to find a place for a people whose yearning burnt in their breasts.

I put my face close to Abu Mashour's. My nose touches his. I feel happy and I smile. I am touched by memories of my past. If I had married that fabulously wealthy man, I would have five children by now. If I had married that man of opulence, I could be touring Europe at this moment, his money in my pocket, and his pot-belly and yellow teeth by my side. All I would have on my mind would be which of the boutiques of London and Paris would be the best place to buy my wardrobe for next season.

How noble for a human being to live for a cause. Only by risking his life can he fulfil his goals. I used to spend my days hiding behind books, behind my family, behind the ideological positions of my party, my friends, my daily contacts and activities. I felt secure hiding behind education and intellect, the comforting resonances of history. I used to be afraid of death because I was afraid of life, but now death doesn't seem like death any more. It is like a beautiful risk, eternal and unaffected, a risk which could end in failure but without which there can be no victory. I am like a tree which can extend her branches to the heavens, carrying in its shade joy and sorrow with every move-ment. I smell the scent of Swiss pine everywhere. I am drowning in a sea of pine. I am free of my fear, of my past, free of death itself. I laugh out loud. Abu Mashour clasps my hand:

"What is it? You haven't gone back to being a poet have you?"

I try to tell him about the thunderbolt which sometimes hits me, like a flash of inspiration which allows me to give a true account of myself. That night I had decided to tell the truth about myself.

We get up. Outside the restaurant we cross the street, walking calmly under the light rain. We talk about everything but the operation. The plan requires that we do not mention it until our mission is fully realised. Clearly our comrades in the leadership were wary of the psychological effects which might result from discussions of that nature.

We arrive at the hotel. The comrade from Germany walks with us to the lift and then bids us goodnight and goes off to his hotel.

In the lift, my face meets Abu Mashour's. I see olive groves in his eyes. I see a nobility in them which belies his living a life of exile. I put my head on his shoulder and feel a strong urge inside me to say something. He strokes my hair and leans down to kiss it, saying:

"Well, my temporary wife, shall we be lovers?"

I hear his voice coming to me clearly as if for the first time. It has the clarity of a song sung by the human voice alone, without any musical accompaniment. A mournful psalm, but one expressing much hope, and, if it were ever used to serenade a woman, it would have the same force as all the love letters ever written, putting into the shade the feeble poems composed by men who spend lazy days under the sun with rich food in their bellies.

We get to our room. The bridal suite for two young people coming from America to spend their honeymoon in Europe. We try to restrict our conversation to the inane yet all-embracing subject matter of the newly-wed. That is how it was planned. There were fears that the room might be bugged or that we were being watched. We try to sleep. The sounds of silence are dispersed in our room like a muffled weeping. I search for sleep. I search for calm. I try to think back to all the stories which my mother used to tell me, and I go over them one by one in my mind. Faces come to me in the darkness. I do not want to close my eyes for fear of losing these moments. Abu Mashour turns over in the bed and faces me. He looks at me through the gloom, which is broken only by the light from the street coming in through the curtains.

"Are you still awake, Nadia?"

We both light cigarettes and smoke them in the dark without talking.

When morning comes we are still in bed. The light streams in. I get out of bed and go towards the window. When I pull back the curtains I see Geneva sleeping in the first hours of daylight. Red roofs slanting towards the lake. The waters of the lake flowing down to the sea, wherever that may be. All things on this planet are going somewhere. And us? There is a knock on the door. The hotel employee comes in with morning coffee and the day's newspapers. I look at the face of the Arab world scowling out at us from the pages of newsprint. Geneva's local paper talks about the likelihood of the US Secretary of State making a visit to one of the front-line Arab states. The *Herald*

Tribune goes on about oil price rises. I turn the pages over and look into the face of haggard, old Europe and her problems. Local elections in France. Health insurance in Italy. The women's movement in Britain.

Abu Mashour watches the expression on my face as I read the item about the Secretary of State over again.

"Well, do you think it will be our heads this time?"

I feel a strange contempt for this universe. Why not hijack planes? Why not bomb them in their companies and corporations? The White House itself. We have to implement these things when facing the illegality which characterises their dealings with us.

Frank . . .

Why am I telling you about all this now? I listen to the drunks. They are singing *Le Temps des Cerises*.

Oh, if the time of cherries returned.

I look at the white pages lying before me like the shrouds of a corpse. I am still here, stuck to my seat in the corner of the café. I want to ask the waiter the name of the café. I call him over and order another glass of cognac. He brings it to me, singing to himself as he comes.

Oh, if the time of cherries returned. If you were here this evening, we could sit on the right bank, close to the Palais de Justice, where the Sa'alik of today, Paris's down-and-outs are sleeping, with nothing but their bottles of wine and their cigarettes. How great to be a Su'luk these days.

If you were here this evening, I could tell you about Abu Mashour, and about Geneva and Ayntab. I could have asked you to go back there with me so that you could cleanse yourself of your pursuit of oblivion. I too would be cleansed, cleansed of my cowardice and my inability to expose my real face to this world. Both of us would become Sa'alik of the revolution, each in his own way. But you've never even heard of 'Urwa bin al-Ward, their leader.

If you were here this evening, we could have both gone there and I would have turned you into a thunderbolt, into the Pole Star. You have to leave these dead pavements behind you, the inertia of this life, traffic jams, rampant capitalism, elections which they use as chips on the gaming tables, this watery sun, your diet of Wagner.

If only you were here this evening! Frank! Please! I need you. I need your arms. I need your chest. I need your eyes. I need you, otherwise I cannot leave Paris. Every one of her streets we used as a rendezvous and every paving-stone has memories for us. I don't want to leave Paris like this. Alone. In the rain. I can't bear it that no one is here to bid me farewell. How harsh it is to be alone in a city.

My mind races into the future. I miss you Frank, but I don't want you back. You fire my intellect, but only the memory of my former comrades causes my heart to palpitate. I try to see into the future. Into the past. Back to the days when I was with them. Why the past and the future always? It's now, at this very moment, that I am here. The night revolts against my sorrow. And the day.

The People. The Cause. The Dream. War. They have all become lost words.

Come back quickly before the woman inside once more surrenders herself to the current which has been carrying her away over the last four years, taking her far away from her homeland. She has lapsed into idiocy, neither loving nor loved, neither a guerrilla nor a veteran. One foot in the Gulf of Alexandretta and the other in Europe.

You are far away from me. Between us lie seas and continents. Ayntab is over there burning in the heart of the sea. The night is long and you are far away. The thought of returning home frightens me. The cold walls. Solitude. My bed. The map of my homeland hanging on the opposite wall like a corpse. Yes, the decomposing corpse of my homeland has been there for some time now. Every day, I open the wooden casket and take a look at the body. Every time I get that instant of joy and elation when I see that it has not completely rotted away yet. My homeland may be dead, but it has not rotted yet. If I can just bury it in your heart I will be able to relax. But there is not enough room in your heart and it will not go anywhere but my eyes. I put it back there and close the lids.

And ever since that day. . . .

Why do we go back to that day. Well, in any case, since that day, if I awake in the morning and cannot find my homeland . . . They tell me that it mounted a horse and rode away, far away . . . I asked after it everywhere. I looked in your body. I looked in the eyes of Raoul. In Ahmad's songs which came from the depths of Upper Egypt. *Layali wa ya layali, wa ah!* In the cup of Adnan which he carries far away to where he buried the names – even the names of the gods. In the Quranic verses and poems which al-Bahi memorised and recited at every opportunity. My homeland is far away. It has mounted a charger and has ridden to heaven knows where.

Suddenly, I call out its name. The rulers' bully-boys heard me and they came and plucked out my eyes. Through the blood which was washing down my body, I saw my homeland fall between my tears, and disappear.

Ever since that day . . .

I have been afraid of going home. The four walls frighten me. I am awakened and the woman-tree is awakened. I say:

"I want to forget. Yesterday they came for my blood from afar. They came from the cities which I have fled from. There they are now, over-running everything. Oh, if the time of cherries returned.

Geneva. Everything is covered in snow. A small grey cat crouches in the corner of our room at the Ritz Hotel. The hotel employee had brought it to the room that morning, a gift from Mme Roseline, the woman who runs the Casino. She saw how fond I was of cats when I played with her Persian during dinner. I was very kind and well behaved with him, just as a civilized young lady coming from America would be. She started a long conversation with me about cats, asking how long I had been interested in them, whether I was attracted to one particular breed more than others, whether I was thinking about having children. At the last question, she winked at me so that Abu Mashour would not see and she whispered:

"You'd better not have children if you really are fond of cats. They get very jealous sometimes, you know."

I reassured Mme Roseline that the cats of the world were completely safe if the matter was in my hands.

I get up and start to put on my clothes. The phone rings and, as I lunge towards it, there is a voice inside me telling me that this might be something to unsettle us in the run-up to the operation – there was only one day to go now. I lift the receiver. It is Saleh, telling me that he and Farhan have arrived in Geneva from Frankfurt an hour before. We decide to meet at the Restaurant Edward VII near the monument to the Unknown Soldier. I finish dressing and run down to the hotel lobby. I find Abu Mashour in one corner having a cup of coffee. His face is filled with consternation. He has not stopped asking questions since we arrived in Geneva. What good would this kind of action do us? Why this war in the sky which can't ever be justified?

The doubts in Abu Mashour's mind caused me to consider whether or not to take him off the team. Maybe I should get another comrade to take his place. But how? We were on the eve of the operation and every discussion we begin always reaches the same conclusion. He was one of the best of guerrilla fighters we had and the bravest of them all, but he did not know how to conduct a political campaign. At university he dropped out in the first year in order to join the military camps.

I go up to him. He carries on staring vacantly at the white blanket of snow on the other side of the glass.

I say to him:

"Saleh and Farhan have arrived from Frankfurt and they're waiting for us at the Edward VII."

He acknowledges what I say and gets up from his place. I look through the thick medical spectacles which he was asked to wear as a disguise during the operation. I do my best to make light of the situation:

"Did you write a will before you left Harran?"

"My only request is that you musn't marry anyone else after my death!"

"What a marvellous feudal lord you would have made. Still not over desire for possession, eh?"

I see a smile illuminating the dark features. Behind his thick glasses his eyes look like those of a Greek god. Yet strangely there is still doubt in them, doubt about everything. I do not know why guerrilla fighters always have doubt in their eyes. Your eyes, Frank, are like two eternal springs of doubt.

Before we cross the street to the overheated restaurant, I say to Abu Mashour:

"You're still not sure about this operation, are you?"

"It's not this operation particularly, it's action outside the Occupied Land in general. I'm sorry but our opinions on this are totally different."

"Well, you better not let Saleh and Farhan see what you're think-ing. If you really don't want to go with us, we could do it without you, you know."

Signs of sadness and dismay appeared on Abu Mashour's face. I had misunderstood his apparent hesitation. He explains to me:

"Nadia, I wouldn't ever let my personal views stand in the way. Of course I'm going with you, and I'll see this task through to the very end. However, I retain the right to disagree with you about how useful the operation will be and what benefits it will bring. The way I see it, what we are doing is indulging in individual heroics to the detriment of the heroism of our whole people. Tomorrow, all the papers will write about Nadia and Abu Mashour and your photograph will prob-ably fill three or four columns on every front page. You'll be a heroine. But while all this is happening, the real heroes, the ones living and dying on the Northern Plains, and in Harran and Ayntab, will not even get a mention."

"But we need the publicity, Abu Mashour. Can't you see? We are surrounded by Western Europe."

"In ten years in Vietnam . . . "

I do not let him finish:

"Don't give me that stuff about Vietnam and Cuba and all the rest of them. Every revolution has its own special circumstances. Our circumstance is that we are fighting without a country, without a legal system, outside the law."

"What about Bolivia?"

"Totally different. As you know, the rebels were slaughtered before anybody came to help them."

"You'll make a great terrorist, you know, Nadia. Have you thought at all about the hundreds of innocent people who are going to be on board that aeroplane?"

His remark gave me a sharp pain in my insides. Ever since Issam had broken the news to me that my life was going to change, I had spent a long time studying various aspects of the operation, and the most difficult thing for me was the passengers. I had lost a lot of sleep, thinking about how we were involving them in our actions. In the end I made a promise to myself that I would do everything in my power to make sure they were spared. And anyway, why shouldn't they be plucked from their dull lives for a while, from their spoilt pets and their capitalist rat-race.

"Abu Mashour, no one has a God-given right to live on this planet in complete safety all the time, particularly when there are millions of others out there dying in conditions of terror and violence. If you want to say what we're doing is terrorism, then by all means, call me a terrorist, one of the best!"

Our discussion is not over by the time we get to the restaurant. We go over to our comrades and greet them with hugs and questions. Then we sit down and have lunch in silence, broken only by the odd remark made by one or other of us. I told them that we were still waiting for two of our comrades whom we were expecting from Hamburg; a Palestinian doctor and an Algerian, the latter being the one who was supposed to be directing the operation until we board the aeroplane. Once on board, command of the operation was to be handed over to me. We finish our meal and head back to the hotel for coffee. When I am outside in the snow and the wind, I feel as if the fog of the previous night has still not been cleared from my breast. I feel a strange kind of delirium. I run to the opposite side of the road without heeding cars coming from left and right which only just miss me. I raise my head and look up to the sky, welcoming the spots of rain as they fall into my eyes. I think of my days in Arum. The chill of autumn. The wilted almond blossoms still clinging to the mother-tree.

The telephonist at the hotel greeted me and told me that a telephone call had come for me from Hamburg a few minutes before. It seemed that the comrades needed to speak to us urgently. I left the group in the lobby and ran out towards the railway station. After buying some bars of chocolate, I asked the shopkeeper where the nearest phone booth was. She pointed to the right without breaking off from her conversation with a customer about the weather and the price of meat. I turned around and looked carefully to see whether anyone had been following me or watching me. When I was certain that the coast was clear, I went over to the booth and closed the door firmly behind me. I dialled the operator and asked for a Hamburg number. Since the beginning of my training for this operation, I had stopped carrying around pieces of paper or note-books with names, addresses or telephone numbers on them. I committed every name and number to memory. Man can do most things when he puts his mind to it.

I hear the voice of my Algerian comrade coming on at the other end:

"Have you had a lot of snow in Geneva?"

"It's been raining since yesterday, actually."

"Is it very cold?"

"Yes, but it would still be very nice to do the trip around the lake. When can you make it here?"

Our conversation is in English. He tells me that the two of them will be arriving in the evening. I terminate the conversation and replace the receiver. There is a momentary feeling of dizziness in my head. The time is nearly upon us. I hurry back to the hotel, stopping at a newspaper vendor to get the morning papers. When I get to the hotel I do not find my comrades in the lobby. I go to the room where Abu Mashour was doing some exercises.

"Where have Saleh and Farhan gone?"

"They went back to their hotel. They said they were feeling a bit tired."

"The other two are going to be here tonight."

Abu Mashour realises from this information that the final date and time of the operation have been decided upon. We are to go the following day.

We sit on the side of the bed and study our charts. We look at the route the flight will take, as well as the altitude and the possible air conditions that we will encounter along the way. I expected some turbulence over Italy. If the weather conditions got too bad we might have to make an emergency landing at Rome Airport. But landing would be risky, especially if we were going to take control of the flight immediately after leaving Geneva Airport. Abu Mashour reminded me that the plane could fly at a lower altitude if the weather conditions demanded it, but I preferred to leave matters of that nature to the afternoon, when Saleh could take the final decision. He had been a pilot, after all, and his knowledge of such things was much wider than ours.

We had been waiting in Geneva for the beginning of the operation for ten days now. On the third day I had sent Issam a telegram which had said:

"Everything is okay. Surgery has had to be postponed three days."
What this meant was that we were going to begin the operation three
days later than previously planned.

Two days later I sent another telegram. This time it read:

"The doctor has advised the commencement of planned treatment.
E.C.T. begins on . . . " and here I specified the exact time and date of
the operation. I finished the telegram with the usual words: "We are
well. Love to you all."

I looked at the word 'well' on the page. It looked like a decomposing
corpse. I tried to believe it myself: We are well. I thought about how,
without realising it, we are governed by clichés and linguistic formulae,
making us slaves to the word although the word has little to do with the
conditions and events of our lives. I handed the telegram over to the
blonde girl who was behind the post office counter and left quickly.

How cold I feel tonight.

Where are you, Frank?

Why is my homeland attacking me with such force tonight? Why
am I weighed down by my conscience, my exile, my desire for life?
What made me take on the life of a guerrilla fighter living in the
realms of covert action, my hand on my gun, the night sheltering me
in her dark corners? I try to convince myself that I had no choice. I
think back to my political activities before I joined the Organization, I
see that all I did was talk.

The night of the Fifth of June again. Endless talk about workers' rights
and the *fellaheen*. Speeches and empty threats from our leaders. War
raining down on Arum and Ayntab. All my peers, my intellectual
guides, my leaders, all as helpless as myself to separate themselves from
the calamity. Coming back from the military hospital, the sight of
civilian victims of a napalm attack fresh in my memory, the smell of
their burning flesh still lingering in my nostrils. I can find no way of
putting them out of my mind and restoring myself to my usual calm,
the eerie calm of the swamps. I go to our exalted leader who never errs.
I knock on his door. His beautiful wife opens it for me, looking like she
has just emerged from the sweet land of her dreams. I tell her I want to
see him.

"He's busy. He didn't get any sleep last night."

I push my way through and find him in his office. I scream at him:

"I've got a score to settle with you. Let's talk! Let's talk about you. Let's talk about where you stand at this moment. Tell me, for instance, how you expected us to drive them back from the gates of Arum when you hadn't given us anything to fight with?"

He looks at me in his condescending way, full of pity and compassion, like a father regarding his wayward child. He says to me, with the wan smile never leaving his lips:

"Nadia, you may be a good poetess but you've got a lot to learn about politics. What you don't realise is, the current situation can be looked at in a positive light. The war has put paid to single party rule. For years the petit-bourgeois Arab governments have been telling us that democratic and social progress cannot be allowed to go ahead until the patriotic battle against Israel has been won. This war has shown up their fundamental inability to achieve that victory and now those idiots will have to accept that they can't stay in power all by themselves. . . ."

At this point I lose all restraint and I scream at him: "I can't take any more of this. I can't stand any more of this ideological clap-trap. Are you seriously asking me to accept the occupation of half my land to prove the validity of some party-political argument? Arum is almost in the hands of our enemy!"

He did not expect an answer like that and I could see the blood draining from his face. I doubt that anyone had ever before contradicted our exalted leader. Never in the history of the party had the finger been pointed at him like that. We were meant to listen to what he said and repeat it verbatim.

I felt lost when I went back out onto the streets. They seemed to stretch away forever. Arum is worn out. Her face is old and tired. I get close to the corner of the fortifications. I see someone I know and I run towards him.

"Ali. What's going to happen, do you think?"

He smiles and asks me:

"How's your poetry going?"

Sometimes the monster inside us rises up. At that moment I felt my blood turn into a storm of hatred. The cobblestones on the road made me think of the number of skulls which had fallen to bring Arum into being, and Arum is now threatened with occupation, or, worse, total obliteration.

Tomorrow Arum will be penetrated by an occupying army. The soldiers will penetrate me and my sisters and my friends and they will sow the seeds of occupation in our wombs. Then the nausea will come and we'll be spewing up our slogans every morning.

I run towards the broadcasting building. I go straight past the guards and soldiers without even looking at them. Breathlessly I climb the three flights of stairs to the door of Bahiya's office. She is a comrade of ours, who comes from one of the Gulf countries. She sees the pallor of my face and the fear in my eyes, and she asks me to come in. She takes a jar of Valium tablets out of her desk and gives one to me:

"Try to calm yourself, Nadia. We've just heard the news. They're on the outskirts of Arum."

I stare at the ground. I felt like going into the studio and speaking to the Arab peoples, those whose hearts were tied to Arum. I would say to them: "Oh mountains of dough and pleasure, here we are harvesting the results of your oil, your mistresses and your great wealth." I would tell them to pray to their saviour to protect them. Pray. Pray hard. Pray to Him for your bodies to be burned and for real men to emerge from your ashes. I wanted . . .

It is raining hard in Paris. The road is narrow. The walk back home frightens me.

Everything is floating in the distance. When you are exiled from your homeland, your whole life drifts away from you. Even you, my love, who is far away, even you are a knife which cuts deep into my flesh and uncovers all the agonies of my past.

My homeland is far away. The homeland in my eyes. Lebanon in June. A black mark on our foreheads that will be there for eternity.

Geneva, once again.

I approach the inspection point at the airport, trying not to let my face show anything that is going on inside my head. I pray that they don't choose this moment to get over-efficient and security conscious. I look at Abu Mashour as he moves ahead in front of me. He looks calm and natural. Saleh and Farhan are behind us standing in a different queue. The plan required that Saleh takes his case and exchanges it with another which had been left in a locker in the duty-free area by an accomplice who worked at the airport. I thought for a moment about our European comrade whom we did not know, the safe houses, the expenses which were met and how crucial the support of such people was to the outcome of our plans.

Abu Mashour passes the inspection point. He is posing as a Mexican and the security official has no cause to think that anything is amiss, previously there has been no threat like us . . . He passes through to the other side and I breathe a sigh of relief. My turn is coming. I have my American passport at the ready. I am also carrying a bundle of English language newspapers which I made sure I had bought that morning. I can hear a tumultuous noise coming from within me and it makes me think of the end of the world. I am afraid that the official might see my homeland written across my face. The besieged and banished homeland that is in my eyes, wherever I go in this world. I am worried that he will notice my dark complexion and ask me where I come from. In the event, however, he merely nods his head when he sees my US passport and waves me through without bothering to put a stamp on my papers. I see that Saleh and Farhan have gone through before me. Walking separately, we head towards the gate and board the aeroplane. Abu Mashour and I sit in adjacent seats. I open my handbag and take out a cigarette. I turn to my comrade and ask him:

"How are you feeling? Are you confident?"

He nods his head and we both breathe out our smoke into the air of the cabin. I look around. It's certainly a beautifully fitted-out plane. Over the entrance to the first-class cabin there is a sign saying 'No Smoking' in English and in Hebrew. On the side panels are pictures of the towns in the Occupied Land. The minutes pass. A hostess comes along the aisle and requests that we extinguish our cigarettes and fasten our safety-belts. The plane takes off. The city appears below us cradled in last night's snow, looking like a bride lost in her dreams. Many brightly coloured flowers are planted around the town and this makes the bride look like a body whose wounds pour out their blood and hatred.

I seek the succour of the cities I love. I look to Arum the Beautiful, who taught me how to breathe and how to live, and how to fight and kill in order to survive. Her beautiful face in the gloom of the morning on which I left her for Harran. There is none more beautiful than she as she pulls back the veil from her face at dawn and smiles at me. Geneva's face disappears in the mist, like the face of a loved one on a station platform. Ten minutes pass. I see clouds, only clouds.

The hostess comes round with drinks, and the fog which I was holding onto slips through my fingers and my lips. I try to stop it, but I fail. I take a glass and rest my head against Abu Mashour's shoulder. The passenger behind us watches and gives a little smile. Perhaps he thinks to himself: "Ah, what a sweet young couple."

The first quarter of an hour passes and I hear the voice of the air hostess welcoming us on board on behalf of the pilot. She informs us that we have passed into Italian airspace and that the aircraft is currently flying at nine thousand feet. Our time has come.

I put my hand down to feel the revolver. A shiver runs down my spine. I take my handbag and get up to go to the toilet. I move along the aisle clutching my tummy, pretending to be suffering from a sudden stomach ache. Abu Mashour goes with me trying to help me. One of the passengers says:

"She should have a hot drink and lie still for a while."

Together we move from the second-class to the first-class cabin. Abu Mashour presses my hand firmly to indicate that I am to go straight to the cockpit. Terrible moments of silence throw their shadow over us while we wait for Farhan and Saleh to reach us. The hostess tries to stop them, saying:

"Please wait a moment, gentlemen. There's a lady through there who is not feeling very well."

They pay no attention to what she says and they continue on their way. When they join us in first-class cabin, I run towards the front of the plane, taking out my revolver with my right hand, I kick open the door of the cockpit, and take out the explosive device with my left hand, priming it to go off once the timer is set. I speak my prepared statement to the crew.

"We are fighters for . . . " Here I say the name of our organization. "This aircraft is now under our control. It will fly to Arum passing over the Occupied Land. The route will be set by us. Any deviation from that course and any false move made by you will oblige us to blow up the aeroplane."

The pilot looked on helplessly, his face like wax. Behind me a struggle broke out between Saleh, Farhan and a couple of passengers. Perhaps they were members of the Israeli security forces. The co-pilot also attempted to put up some resistance, but Abu Mashour took care of him and tied him to his seat. We heard a gunshot and one of the Israelis fell to the ground, Saleh overpowered the other one and tied him up. Farhan told the passengers to stay in their seats, then read out the text of our statement and told them:

"We mean you no harm. We do not want to have to resort to violence. All we want is for the whole world to know about our cause." After that they gave a brief outline of the history of Palestine and the Palestinian question to the passengers.

I sit glancing at the radar screen every once in a while, keeping the barrel of my gun pointed at the pilot's head. A distant desire for life tugs at my consciousness. We must not blow up this plane if we can help it. We must conserve the lives of the passengers if at all possible.

I give our demands clearly to the captain.

"Condition One: – the release of a woman freedom fighter who is being tortured in Nablus.

"Condition Two: – the release of four of our comrades captured during an operation on the Northern Plains.

"Condition Three: – the release of five people recently arrested during a demonstration in Jerusalem.

"These demands must be met or we will have little choice . . . we will blow up the plane and all the passengers on it."

The pilot nodded his head in silence. After some minutes he asked me whether I wanted him to tell the air traffic control at Rome Airport about our demands. I nodded in agreement but added:

"As long as you don't try anything."

Over Rome, which was sunk in the arms of its hills, I noticed that the plane had lost altitude. I looked at the altimeter and it was clear that we were now flying much too near to the ground. I saw the game the pilot was playing and I brought the gun closer to his head.

"Listen to me. We're not children. Just tell them our conditions and that we have changed our direction. Don't forget, I won't hesitate to kill you if necessary. I have a comrade on board who is capable of flying this aircraft to its destination."

He nodded emphatically and relayed the instructions to the control tower with a plea to his government to accept our conditions. I felt a shiver running through my body. My eyes were fixed on the instrument panel, without looking away for one moment. We were a whisker away from death, and I was thinking how much I wished the war could be over. I wanted time to stand still. I wanted to open my eyes and find myself under one of the green olive trees on the outskirts of the seaside town where I was born. I wanted to stretch out on the ground and stare up into the blue sky. I looked at the calm face of my comrade, who had remained silent all the time, and I saw the resolve in his eyes.

The plane circled the skies above Rome Airport for nearly a quarter of an hour. We were waiting for an answer from the control tower at the airport. I had given them a time limit of twenty minutes to come back to us with their reply. After a quarter of an hour, a cypher was received, their answer that they were not able to get a reply from the embassy did not convince me and I took this to mean that they had rejected our demands. I ordered the pilot to head for Athens and not to tell the control tower at Rome where we were going. I did, however, tell him to leave them in no doubt that regardless of where we ended up our conditions were not going to change.

Time passed slowly. Each second seemed a lifetime. Each minute an epoch. Complete silence prevailed in the aircraft. It seemed as though we were in a moment of humility before God, as though we were all about to die. It is hard to be the killer, and humiliating to be the one killed. Why do we fight wars? Why do we manufacture weapons? Why do we cause death?

I didn't go far with my questions. I thought of the million-and-a-half refugees at risk from death, not from war, but of hunger. A million-and-a-half people sitting shivering under canvas on rain-swept nights. Women who give birth out of their fear for extinction. I thought about what it means to be Palestinian and to live the Palestinian dilemma which says you either live the harsh life of an exile or you learn how to kill.

I took a deep breath and felt my hand on the explosive device. It was as though my comrades and I were on board a ship which could not find a place to dock, with a crew which had no hope. The souls of one hundred and fifty passengers rest on my shoulders and conserving their lives was a concern to me, but I also had to think of my displaced people.

At that moment Abu Mashour puts his face close to mine and says:

"If we get out of this alive, I'll always love you, you know."

The distances are erased and I feel time like a black spot eating up my memory.

I replied:

"I'll always love you too."

How terrible it is that we are lovers at the very moment of death. Our lives in those awful seconds were hostages to any mistake which we, or the pilot, or the passengers might make. Where were all the 'Fathers', the leaders and the theorists. They should stop making their resounding speeches for a while and be made to live through terrible moments like these. Oh my forefathers . . . our present leaders call themselves 'Abu this' and 'Abu that' but they are only fathers of sterility and impotence. I tell myself that it is not death we seek, but it feels like death when death is so close to you. I looked at the pilot's face at that instant. He was in his mid-forties and his face was a typical Middle Eastern face. He had the same haughtiness which seems to be there in our features and which, under the hot sun, turns us all into people lost in our dreams. I felt a desire to talk to him:

"You know what, I think you were born in Palestine and I bet your father was a Palestinian Jew."

Cultivated in Palestine, his offspring born on its soil, and there he had known nights of hunger and thirst just as we did.

Before we got to Greek airspace, the captain turned to me and stared at me for some time, examining my face. Finally he said to me in Arabic:

"We're nearly over Greece now. Shall I transmit your conditions to Athens Airport?"

I hesitated for a moment. I thought that landing in Nicosia – if we were pushed – would be easier because of the smaller number of security men there.

"Nicosia. You will fly directly to Nicosia."

The aircraft continued on its course.

Before our descent at Nicosia Airport, Saleh came up to me in the cockpit and told me that one of the female passengers was feeling airsick. I told him to give her one of the pills which were in a bottle in my bag. He took the bottle and went out of the cockpit without saying a word.

Soon afterwards we landed at Nicosia and told the passengers to keep their safety-belts fastened and not to move from their seats.

I stared blindly at the control panels while Abu Mashour stood behind the pilot with the revolver.

Despair. Again the enemy government refuses to comply with our demands. It was simple then. Somehow I had to get us to the airport at Arum. I looked at the pilot. I could see from his expression that the stress was beginning to have an effect on him. I considered asking Saleh to take his place at the controls, but then decided not to for fear of upsetting the balance of the operation.

It was getting hotter inside the plane and the noise coming from the passengers increased. There were cries coming up from all corners asking us to allow them to get out of the plane. But we were all prisoners at that moment: the four of us, the passengers, the pilot and cabin-crew. I told the pilot to take us to Arum. Something inside me told me that the authorities at Arum would not allow us to land and doubt was eating away at my insides. Would they allow their land to be used as the stage in this first and strangest airline hijacking operation undertaken by the Palestinian resistance movement. Up until a few days before, we had been nothing but a historical joke which the world thinks will not continue – and we would have ended where we began, like so many other similar revolts between the years 1936 and 1948 in the Occupied Land.

"Fly us over the Occupied Land."

He hesitated for a moment. I told him again more forcefully. He taxied the aircraft round and we were off again. Nicosia Airport looked hardly bigger than the palm of my hand under the sunshine. Beautifully ordered rows of houses and gardens stretching down towards the sea, which looked hot and clear as it lapped at the feet of the town. I thought of the Arab towns just over the horizon. The sound of the voices died down and all was quiet again inside the cabin. Expectation and a wish for deliverance could be felt in the air.

Soon we saw the houses of the Occupied Land, small and strung together in lines. A green strip which marked the coast was calmly bathed in the waters. Down there Abu Mashour was born. Down there my friend Mahmoud was writing poetry on every surface he could find, on the trees, on the mountains of Carmel, on the sea . . .

"Haifa," said the pilot, totally unmoved by what we saw below. I thought of Mahmoud's face at the Youth Conference in Belgrade when I criticized him for agreeing to be a delegate in the official Israeli group. I was filled with pain and frustration. I lowered my face so that the pilot could not see the waves of sorrow which were passing over me at that moment. Mahmoud, it is ordained that we must pass you with death by our sides.

I saw him again in Paris in 1973 on his way back from Moscow. I reminded him of our meeting in Belgrade. Light spots of rain were falling on my cheeks and anxiety overcame me, just as it always does when the rain falls. We walked across the Place Saint Michel together and sat down at the first café table which we could find. I did not tell him about the silent message which I sent down to him in the Occupied Land that day, as I was passing overhead in a plane carrying us to the heart of the sorrows of the Arabs.

Shortly after we had crossed the coastline, I heard the pilot speaking to the ground in Hebrew. There were two specks behind us on the radar screen. Abu Mashour translated what the pilot had said then told him, also in fluent Hebrew, to warn the control towers of the airfields which we were going to pass that any plane following us would put the passengers in great danger.

"If any aircraft comes close to us we will blow up this plane and everyone on it."

It was clear that the pilot did not expect anyone to be able to speak Hebrew. I heard him repeat in English what Abu Mashour had said to him. At that moment two Mirage jet-fighters, which had been shadowing us, dived back down towards the ground. When I realised the game which the pilot had been trying to play, I said to him:

"Listen. If you try to trick us, we'll kill you. I don't want to blow up this plane, but I shan't hesitate to do so if I have to. I hope you are clear on this point. Fly us to Arum and tell your airfields what will happen if they send anything to follow us or to get in our way."

A moment of eternity. A moment of death. The songs that soldiers sing as they are marching to war are the most heartwarming and rousing songs there are. But fighters like us cannot sing. They can't even whisper. They are bound to silence and secrecy.

The sea seemed to be like many different seas which have come together over time. I saw, or thought I saw, the waves pounding down into the shore. How Arab I feel at that moment. I see the face of Mahmoud Darwish on the face of the sea and in the trees. The air in the cabin was cheerless, a strange, unavoidable gloom. The notion of death came to me once again. I was reminded that revolutionaries do what they do because of their love of life. However, because they love life they have to expose themselves to death. Abstractions take on corporeal forms because death can come to us at any time and so celibacy is impossible for us. In fact, we are the opposite of the Nazarene when he rejects the kiss of Mary Magdalene on his feet. As far as I was concerned, to volunteer to go to your death was an irrational act. That is why our reasons for doing so are also irrational.

The plane gets to the sky over Arum and I see her beauty behind the clouds and the trees. I see her eyes being opened and her arms spread out to hug me to her breast. I, who had left her without so much as a goodbye. I send a message to the control tower asking them to allow us to land. When the reply comes it is in the negative.

Again I was refused permission but we had no choice: we were almost out of fuel and the passengers were in no condition to fly on to another destination. Added to this was the fact that one of our strategic goals since the beginning of this operation was to land at Arum. We wanted them to sit up and take notice of us. This Arab state had talked about the liberation of Palestine for the last quarter of a century but in truth they did nothing. They turned a noble and tragic cause into something to distract their people with, a bartering piece to use against their enemies. Not one of those leaders forgets to mention the old cliché in every speech he delivers whatever the occasion: "It is our sacred duty to support Palestinian resistance by every means and we are doing everything possible in the service of liberation." But we know the extent of hollow rhetoric, lies and delusion that is in those words. And we well know the number of our comrades who are imprisoned in their gaols, and we know the truth of their attitude to the struggle. But here we were in the sky over Arum. The dispute between ourselves and the airport authorities was still going on. Ever since we had entered their airspace we had been receiving warnings that we would not be able to land at Arum Airport. We held a quick and heated discussion and made some inevitable decisions. We would have to land under any circumstances even if it led us all to our deaths. My voice was a mixture of the cold, hard tones of the guerilla tinged with a desperate hope that they would see things our way. I spoke to the airport authorities:

"We are unable to continue flying to another location. If you decide not to let us land, we couldn't make it anywhere. This aircraft will drop out of the sky."

Hard tense moments passed, like those rare moments in which time becomes more dense, when the stages of life, and of personal and social history become shortened. The answer came from the control tower – permission had been refused for a second time. The reason was clear, the implications of allowing this capital to be used as the stage for this hijack were as obvious to the authorities as they were to us. I asked to talk to a government representative, one was at hand, as I had expected, because his voice came to me straight away. I told him that the matter was crystal clear and that there were very few choices, we either landed the plane or we would blow it out of the sky. If they forced us to take the suicide solution then the responsibility would be their's alone. I told him that Israel would not be very grateful, nor would its powerful friends, for this bloody decision they would be forcing us to take.

While this conversation was going on between me and the government representative, Abu Mashour noticed that the runway above which we were circling was occupied by army Jeeps to prevent us from landing. I repeated my demand that we be allowed to land, the tension in the official's voice was clear, as he made the biggest decision of his life and granted permission for our landing. I requested that the vehicles be removed immediately. As the Jeeps withdrew the pilot slowly entered into his descent on the runway. A free empty stretch appeared before us, enough for us to execute a safe, calm landing on the tarmac of Arum airport. As we touched down the runway soon became a jungle of police and security vehicles.

Did it all happen very quickly or were things going on outside the normal measures of time? In those moments caught between sky and earth my comrades and I lived a strange mixture of moments of anxiety and self-doubt coupled with seconds of conviction and absolute faith in a goal and a cause. I looked at the passengers, they stared out of the window their eyes full of the demons of terror and mounting hysteria. Some of them sat in a state of near-catatonia, others let out strangled sobs, while some talked frantically to each other.

The jet engines stopped turning and that deep silence which comes after a violent storm took control of the plane. I was back in contact with the government representative:

"We have allowed you to land on condition that the plane is vacated peacefully and that no one is hurt. The plane must also be left intact."

I told him that we were preparing to do that and asked him to order the airport authorities to bring the stairways necessary for the passengers to descend, on the condition that no one tried to board the aircraft. A few minutes later airport workmen had fixed the stairs to the fore and aft doors. I still held the bomb with my finger on the safety catch as Saleh and Farhan helped the passengers to leave the plane in an orderly and calm manner, ensuring that there was no panic. Abu Mashour stayed in the cockpit keeping an eye on the pilot and co-pilot.

I heaved a sigh of relief when I saw the passengers put their feet on the tarmac. I was overtaken by an indomitable cool-headedness which I had not known for a long time. Our task was now less complicated. The instructions were clear, it was necessary, to show that we were serious, for us to blow up the plane. I returned to talking to the government official:

"We have carried out the first part of our agreement, which was to let the passengers leave plane safely. We shall not, however, be complying with the second condition. The instructions from our commanders require that we blow up this plane. Please withdraw all security vehicles from the proximity of the plane or we will kill our remaining hostages "

The government official was astonished and tried to reason with me. The time for reasoning was past. We had kept the pilot and co-pilot with us, we needed some bargaining counter to prevent the authorities taking action against us. Abu Mashour came out of the cockpit behind the two pilots, whose hands were tied and resting on their heads. Quickly we went down the steps one after another, Saleh, Farhan, the pilot, the co-pilot, Abu Mashour and myself. I had left the explosive device, primed to go off, at the front of the aircraft. When we reached the bottom of the stairs we sprinted and caught up with the other passengers, mingling with them in the confusion. A few metres before we reached the airport buildings the explosion we were expecting ripped through the air. We were all thrown to the ground by the force of the blast.

My breath hit the cold tarmac and bounced back up into my face. My eyes were fixed on the body of the burning aeroplane, plumes of black smoke, the colour of the depths of the ocean rose into the sky. Memories tugged at me . . . The memory of the operation . . . The memory of time . . . The memory of the struggle . . . The roar of the explosion was still ringing around the plain where the airport stood. Thick smoke enveloped everything as it billowed into the sky. My breath came back to me off the tarmac. But inside me, at the very core of my being, I felt a strange sense of calm, an inexplicable tranquility.

Oh for a return to the time of cherries.

I feel tired. It is the last part of the night. The café is closing its doors. Old Paris has slept through another long night. All her doors and windows are shut tight. The solitude of the pavements is my homeland. All my friends are tucked up in their beds next to the warm bodies of their pampered wives. Yesterday I met Muhammad, the rancorous Ambassador of Hate, in a café on the Champs Elysées. He chatted to me about his home country, snoring away in blissful sleep, about the trials and tribulations of being an intellectual in that country, about exile and homelessness, and, most of all, and this is the hardest thing for us, we spoke about the reality of Arabs like ourselves whom our fellow countrymen have begun to disown. I joked with Muhammad:

"What would you think of being crowned the king of the Sa'alik. You'd be able to say that your blood was *halal* in every country in the Arab world."

He responded with complete seriousness:

"And when they set a date for my execution, you can be my heir!"

"Do you think they would finish you off in one go? On the contrary, they would make the most of it, cutting you up slowly into little pieces and then throwing a party to celebrate their victory."

Muhammad laughed and changed the subject.

"Where are you now?"

I stood up and said to him:

"As you can see, I am on one of the pavements of exile."

I felt the need to cry at that moment, and I was afraid that I might put my head on his chest and we would cry together.

Frank . . . I can feel death.

Frank . . . I can feel exhaustion creeping all through my body.

Frank . . . Paris is so beautiful in the shadow of silence, but you are far away. I remember you, Frank, at the moment we said goodbye at the airport, just before you flew to another continent. You inclined your head over me and whispered:

"Please wait for me, Nadia. You don't have to be faithful to me, but please wait. If you feel the need to forget, go down to the River Seine and bathe your body in the waters."

Can we forget? Can we really do that? I hear the roar of explosions in the silence of the night. I shiver. The town suddenly becomes an airport and the skies are filled with mist. I see shiny new aeroplanes being flown by women like myself in the middle of the night. I hear explosions. I see your face. I see the face of Abu Mashour, submerged in sorrow and depression. I am tortured by the cold. How I long for you! How I long for your eyes which seem like two oceans. Your face. Why must we see the faces of those we love at times like these? Isn't our losing them hard enough in itself?

My hand touches the place where the bullet went into me during that last operation I was involved in. One of them managed to get me and I was put in irons in a prison in West Germany. I was there for three months. They tortured me. They put so much electricity through my body they practically made my eyes light up. They grabbed my hair and banged my head against the wall, to try to make me confess the names of those responsible for the organization of the operations which I took part in. At that time I pleaded to all of the martyrs to give me strength.

In my mind I held a picture of Ammar bin Yasir, the first martyr of Islam, and father to all martyrs who came after him. I pictured him lying there on the sands of Mekkah, pinned down by a huge boulder, but still refusing to renounce his faith. It was this noble picture of humanity which helped me to bear the pain with fortitude, allowing my comrades to carry on raising international awareness in our cause, and giving them a chance to attempt to rescue me from behind prison bars.

You tell me to forget, but you, of all people, know how hard it is to forget.

Let us not change the subject, though. I love you. But time has changed. I say that I love you, but my voice comes back to me alone without an echo. After him, I couldn't love anyone else. All I was doing, when I gave myself up to the bodies of other men, was looking for peace.

Abu Mashour . . .

All is darkness on the Northern Plains. He kissed me and then left, and he never came back. There is no one who can tell me whether he is alive or dead. I am still waiting, a widow of forbearance and affection. Tell his dark eyes and his broad shoulders that I am still waiting for them. His hands caked in the earth. His rugged features . . . His blood . . . I am still waiting.

Here I am a bullet weakened by grief. I am still alive only because I am unable to find my death. I eat. I drink. I sleep . . . I love you. I try to love you, but I am waiting for him to come back. I pass through stations on long journeys. I live with expectation, and, wherever I am, I repeat his name over and over again.

Your flat on the Place Dauphine. We are fighting against the cold. We become one body which counters the face of the cold. You lift your head to me and say:

"Were you married?"

I smile as I put the picture of your daughter back in its place on the table. I do not reply to your question.

"Why don't you answer me? Remember what you said to me once? That day we went to the Café Saint Claude."

March was moaning outside. The morning rays of the sun stream in through the window. They carry with them the smell of the river. It was the day of my birthday.

"Yes, I was once. But I don't really remember anything about it."

"What? How can you forget something like that? Did you love him?"

"I just used to live with him while I was trying to forget."

"What were you trying to forget? It wasn't one of those arranged marriages was it? You weren't in a harem or something, were you?"

"Don't be silly. It was just an ordinary marriage. I chose him really. It was like an escape for me. Although it turned into my prison."

You are silent. The moment is wasted. You go back to your questions.

"You must have been pretty young when you got married. Come here and tell me a little about your life. You know, I still hardly know anything about you."

"Please Frank, don't let's dwell on the past. I'm here now, with you. That's enough isn't it?"

A whole year has gone by. We have discovered each other's bodies and the nature of time together. In fact it was just about a year ago that we met in a lecture hall at the university, a year ago that we set off on the journey of life together. Two ships going wherever the wind took us, not knowing what lay ahead, or if indeed there was anything ahead. Two ships lost in a salty sea. If we stayed afloat all we had to drink was brine and if we went down, the sharks were waiting for us below.

I talked a lot about my father. About my ancient blood. About the trees. About the old lies which they baptized me with. I told you about my mother's face and her constant prayers, her passionate prayers. Her saviour isn't like anyone else's god. He is merciful and loving and tender. He lives in the forest and among the waves of the sea. He feeds the children and spares the rod from their backs. How serene life was for my mother.

But I did not tell you about my past. I did not tell you of my life with the struggle. I did not tell you about the Palestinians. I never told you about the open wound in my side which never heals. Nor did I tell you that I tried to seek oblivion in the bodies of men. Fleeing from you and to you. Between you and my past. Paris. Exile. You. For a time you were my homeland while I was waiting for the real thing.

I come over to your side of the bed. I put my cheek next to yours. I kiss you and then get out of bed to go to your study. I begin writing a letter to my mother. Your voice calls out:

"Have you really forgotten about your husband?"

"Yes, Frank. I've forgotten everything. Yesterday I bumped into this man in La Coupole. I tried to think where I had seen him before. Suddenly, I realised. I'd seen him in bed. He was my ex-husband."

I heard a quiver in your voice.

"You frighten me sometimes, you know."

I stopped writing and started to read the book which lay open in front of me on the desk. I become engrossed in the words and phrases. I am no longer aware of what is around me. I go over towards the window and open it. I start mouthing meaningless expressions. You look over and realise that I have gone off into a world of my own. Your questions cease, we lapse into silence.

If I had been able to own up to my weakness there and then, I could have told you everything. I used to be a fighter, a 'terrorist'. I was forced to withdraw from the field of combat because of my wounds. But the morning dew rose within me, causing me to sigh. I thought back to the prison vaults where I was tortured.

"Frank, I'm here because I can't be there."

You have come close to me. You pull my head towards your chest and stroke my hair, and you reply:

"My dear little demagogue. Thank you so much for that dazzling insight into your condition." You carry on for a while in this sarcastic vein, "You are right. Why should I search for your past? Isn't it enough that you are here with me now? It's not as though you were some fearsome terrorist who went around hijacking aeroplanes."

I could hardly believe that you had spoken those words. I turned towards the wall so you did not see the blood rushing to my cheeks. I tried to laugh out loud, anything to eclipse that moment of discovery.

Another time at your house on the Place Dauphine.

Your hand touches my hair, which is hanging loosely over my shoulders, wet after the drizzle.

"What is it that you want from me," you say.

I answer quietly and calmly:

"I don't know. Maybe a fellow traveller."

Your face changes to sadness.

"Well, my intransigent friend, what if I told you that I loved you?"

"Then I would ask you to come with me to the Middle East. We would start a revolution there using the methods advocated by you."

Your face turns to anger and you shout at me:

"You're mad. You don't still believe that stuff, do you?"

I was amazed:

"Of course I do. As far as I am concerned, what you wrote then was the best thing you, or anybody, has written on the subject."

"But since the Congo, I have renounced every one of those principles. You can't send people to their deaths like that. It's cheap robbery of the lives of men. It's not heroism, it's butchery. You can't make history in the cauldron. It takes continuity, progression, peace. How long does it take to make a man? Twenty years? Well, it only takes one bullet and he's gone."

"Whose history are you talking about, Frank? Europe? France? You had your revolution here two hundred years ago. In the Third World we are still waiting for ours. We have to change the status quo."

This time you show real anger:

"But that's not the way to do it. History takes its own course. You've tried using force in the Middle East, and look what happened. Do you think that putting a gun to the head of an airline pilot and telling him to fly wherever you want, terrorising hundreds of innocent people, killing, do you think any of that has altered the course of history? Are the conditions in your country any better now? Has anything changed? Of course not! Your fighters just became pirates."

Although you know nothing of my past, I feel the finger pointed at me. The guerrilla fighter's spirit stirs in my blood.

"Palestinian 'terrorists' in other words."

"You know perfectly well what my views are on that matter. The Palestinians and all the others who have . . . "

"Please don't start, Frank. You know as well as I do that you can't impose the values and laws of safe, comfortable Western Europe on a people who have lost their land."

I can see you are about to answer but suddenly I lose control of the anger which has been building up inside me.

"It was Europe that threw Palestine out into the cold. It was Europe that turned her into the harlot she's become today, hanging around the margins of the international community, begging for her crust of bread and offering her meagre wares. It's Europe that's done all that. So don't be surprised if we come along and turn Europe into a shithole."

This drives you mad.

"Look, I spent five years of my life pushed against the walls of a prison. I paid dearly for the mistakes that I made in my revolutionary days. And look what happened in Central America. Look how the revolution has failed the people there. Anyway, I'm French. I'm going to live in France, and from now on my struggle will be to change the situation in France."

"Oh how proud you must be of your dear France!"

"Yes I am."

"And Algeria, and Vietnam, and the bombardment of Damascus? A fine example to revolutionaries the world over, I'm sure."

"It's true, I used to be ashamed of what my country did. I used to be ashamed of the torture and persecution. But now I realize that for all its faults France is better than most at defending individual human freedom."

Silence settles upon us, a silence emanating from a distant star. Our heads become detached from our bodies, from our past. We can't talk about the past, yet we can barely take our eyes away from it. The silence plays tricks on my imagination. I feel that we are in the middle of a huge open space. Night and day are torn to shreds within us in this unknown land. If only we could leave Paris behind us now, returning only when we are old and grey. We would drink in this great human civilization as we drink from our glasses of cognac at the 'Marlein'.

The telephone rings like a young puppy barking for its breakfast. Who could be calling us at that early hour of the morning? I hurry towards the phone and the voice of Olivier greets me:

"Hello. Is that Nadia? Can I speak to Frank, please?"

Before I have time to say anything, he continues:

"Do you know who this is?"

I knew all right; Olivier, the millionaire socialist, with his palaces and his fortunes. I wondered what new deal there was to be made from the struggle this time. I did not answer him but signalled to you to come and take the telephone.

As I get dressed, I listen to you massacring your past in the other room, crucifying it on the wall of a temple before the gathered faithful who prostrate themselves before it. The deity looks down at them from the sky and laughs. You are temple, gods and prayers. A past betrayed.

A comrade stabbed on a sultry tropical night . . . the flaming green of the banana groves.

"Yes, Olivier, I am still writing my memoirs about my time in prison." Then you add: "Nadia's fine. She's started to become interested in African history."

The conversation carries on. I remember Olivier's face on the day we met at the Tour d'Argent restaurant, the face of a war profiteer, with that infuriating grin on his lips making me want to scream. You introduced us, smiling broadly:

"This is Olivier, our favourite socialist millionaire."

I shook my head that day. I could not see how someone could be a socialist and a millionaire at the same time. However, the woman-tree had not been reawakened at that time. We were still in the beginning of our relationship and the desire to forget was carrying me before it like a wild horse. The next time we met was at Clara's house, surrounded by your friends, the career revolutionaries, the writers, the poets talking of anything but poetry, and the beautiful women, their skins exuding the beautiful smells of decadence. I was out of place among all of you and I spent most of the evening in a profound silence. I looked at those faces which lived in the comfort of the towns of ease and irresponsibility. Then Olivier came over to me and like the crass, knownothing he was, said:

"So, why are you so concerned about Irish republicanism then."

Clara pressed my hand and laughed that laugh of hers, like the beating of African drums:

"Don't take any notice of Olivier. He is a film director, absolutely mad and terribly rich. His daddy owns the largest military shipyard in France."

I escaped from Olivier and went and stuck by your side. That day I found out that arms manufacturers also enjoy music and painting, and the company of retired revolutionaries like yourself.

On the way back home from Clara's, I said to you:

"I just don't understand it. How can you, a revolutionary, bear to associate with a merchant of death like Olivier? Isn't that taking conciliation a bit too far?"

With your usual detachment, you reply:

"Do you think that I should spend all my time with workers and revolutionaries? To tell you the truth I find it very hard to mix with them or to gain their confidence completely. They dismiss me as an intellectual. They spurn me."

Olivier carries on talking to you on the phone. Maybe he is going on about new wars for his frigates to fight, or films, or music, or perhaps the latest exploits of his fabulously wealthy father. I go back into your study. My eyes look at you behind the table. Your head is between your hands and it looks as though the telephone is blowing cigarette smoke out into the room. I start listening in to the conversation:

"At the weekend . . . no . . . no . . . the book's coming out at the end of the month . . . what? . . . about my time in the Congo . . . yes . . . when I was in prison . . . oh . . . no, not at all . . . lucrative? Not very, I'm afraid, and the publishers weren't exactly behind me on this one . . . what? . . . a trip at the weekend . . . in your yacht . . . yes, lovely . . . I'll bring Nadia along, but don't talk about you know what, okay . . . She still remembers that time you met at Clara's flat . . . No, my dear Olivier, no. She's just an old pupil of mine . . . yes, very left wing indeed."

I am sitting on the sofa across from your study and I stare at you. My eyes are fixed on your face. Your head is bowed in your hands. You looked like that when they captured you in the country which was just about to erupt in revolution. The photo of you after you were arrested, when you left your comrades in the jungle. The photo of you in the court-room surrounded by your lawyers, who had come from all corners of the world to defend you. You symbolized defiance of death. That picture is there on your wall, your face unblemished, like that of a child. It is there before my eyes hanging on the wall behind your desk, the desk where you have probably just made a deal with one of the greatest of the class exploiters of our time, whose defence you always come to. I close my eyes, Frank, and I push the real picture away from me. I think back to the night when we came out on a demonstration for you, raising our cracked and tired voices in belief and love, demanding that you be allowed to defend yourself. I remember the blood on the street, and those who fell, their eyes still looking up to you. The memory burns me. I feel something choking in my throat. My head spins. I see, on one side, millions of veteran revolutionaries, their heads in their hands, and on the other a judge tries them for their pasts and their present. They give in and are carried away by the current.

Why were you holding your head in your hands? It is as though I see you for the first time, sitting there like that talking to Olivier. Time and distances and men have disappeared . . . I felt my past and my present being consumed in the flames.

I went up to you, filled with madness and anxiety. I pulled your head out of your hands. I went up to the wall with my rage making the blood boil in my veins. I tore down a drawing of you in court. It showed you with your face in your hands while everyone else in the court was looking towards you. I screamed at you:

"You have no right to put your head in your hands like that. You are spoiling one image with the other. Negotiate if you have to, but my dear Marxist, at least choose a different pose."

My voice betrays me. I look at the old mariner on the wall as he battles against a wave on one of the seven seas. I wish the sea would become inflamed and I wish the room which supports us would ignite. At that moment all the energy of the world was used up. I held up a knife, the one you use for opening letters. I plunged it into the breast of the poor old sailor. I dismember the sorry continents which are crucified on your walls. You look at me in amazement. Quickly you say goodbye to Olivier and hang up the phone.

You call out my name, but I do not answer. I can't hear any more. The sound of gunfire has returned to haunt my ears, my eyes and my body. I become a thing of lead and silence. I run towards the door ignoring your questions. I burst out onto the street, into the town, towards the River Seine. I run like a madwoman. A bullet of rage and silence. At the first shelter I come to, I throw myself down on a stone bench and listen to the sound of my sobs mixing with the cry of the autumn winds. I cry as I think back to your past. I cry as I think of what you have become. I cry and kiss the face of Abu Mashour which comes to me from the past. Only then do I feel the tension being lifted from me.

You had finished with me at that moment. I felt a heavy weight falling from my shoulders. It was as if I had been trying to stand between you and your past and to liberate you from yourself, to restore the old face which you used to have . . . In short it was as if I had to save Frank from Frank. The Frank who inflamed my conscience with his words, who made me ask questions about future revolution and how we could make it happen in the Third World. The Frank whom I met after the years of European 'civilization' had killed him off, after he agreed his cease-fire with the bourgeoisie, while the rest of the world erupted in screams and conflagrations. Nothing looks like anything any more. No picture looks like its subject. Between reality and imagination there lies a wasteland of untruth, hypocrisy and treachery. We are just a bunch of naïve fools who believe everything that we hear. Why did I believe all the things which they taught me in school, and everything that the political parties told me, and the secret organisations? Why did I believe that heroism lies waiting in the hearts of men? Everything is just a vain grasping at shadows. Heroism is a big lie which we must believe in. Courage is a smaller lie which we use to wipe out our weakness and our cowardice. Love is a crime which covers the imperfections of possessiveness, selfishness, desire and subjugation. Everything falls. Everything was finished at that moment. Do I still believe everything that I am told? Do I still believe that this planet is a fit place for song, for joy, for making love?

I shout out loud, vainly trying to make excuses for you, the myriad excuses which I am looking for, for you but primarily for myself.

"There is a dispute between you and your comrades . . . You can't go on with them . . . You do not share the same concepts of revolution . . . Your position is an honourable one . . . You don't accept being made into a cheap tool of the media . . . The revolution ended when its leaders started to make compromises . . . You have lost part of your life and you need to search for yourself."

All these excuses are waiting there in my memory, still lined up ready for use, as they were on the day that I decided to split with my comrades. The day I left them under the flames of Ayntab. The day I abandoned them to become the wife of a man as beaten as myself. Abu Mashour's tanned body was blown to pieces. His arms and legs were thrown through the air and here I am looking for peace. But I can smell his rotting remains. I can feel the rags of his clothes pulling me towards the bars and the hashish smokers. Here I am, a coal of revolt which burns no more. And you? The stage where so many revolutions were played out. The masks have fallen now, haven't they? The gods have spoken. Yes, I still believe in the gods, in miracles. I need to believe in them so that I can escape from the hell that is your arduous silence. A tramp comes up to me and asks me, through the wine fumes, for a few coins so that he can get drunk and see Paris as a field of joy. I put my hand in my bag and look for some change, the remains of the compromises we make with this world. I fish out a few coins and give them to this most respectable of drunks. At least he is more respectable than the lapsed revolutionaries and fugitives of forgetfulness whom I normally mix with. He takes the money and disappears. I gather up my body, my face, my failure, and I set out to Place Saint Michel. At the Gilbert Bookshop I see a familiar face. Could that be Ahmad, so early in the day? No doubt he was on the hunt for Marx. Once he's had a couple of whiskies he'll start wanting to kill him. His face made me nervous in the past. I was very much confused by the dreams which he drew from within himself like legends, and which he threw back at us once he gets drunk. He comes up to me and says:

"Nadia, what are you doing up at this hour? We normally only see you when the night is drawing to a close."

I do not answer. I remain silent. He follows me to the street corner.

"What's the matter with you, Nadia?"

He takes hold of my arm and we cross at the traffic-lights. He takes me into a café which is thronging with labourers. I sit down on an old wooden seat. I hear Paris breathing in my chest. Factory smoke and petrol fires. The waiter comes over. He asks for my order.

"A glass of cognac, please."

Ahmad looks at me with surprise.

"Since when have you started drinking at this time of the morning? You haven't turned into an old drunk like me, have you?"

Oh, if Ahmad only knew that I had actually turned into a bullet, but a bullet which is incapable of action. If only he knew that now I held everything in my hand: the world, my homeland, my own body; but all I can do is kill them. I have lost. It is all over.

I lift my glass and cry out:

"Your health, Ahmad. Let's kill our old pal Karl Marx. Let's do it our way."

Do you know Ahmad? I think you met him once at my place. He was getting drunk and talking about Hegel. About Che Guevara. About Frankfurt. He started talking about the Palestinians, and Beirut, and his struggle. Then he dived into a glass of whisky and never came back. You must remember him. Ahmad is like all the disasters of the Arabs rolled into one. I remember, after we had spent an evening together with him, you told me that he was a complete scoundrel. You said he would keep talking and talking and end up never writing anything. To write you need to have silence, you said. Yes, indeed, Frank. To write you need conspiracy, and for conspiracy you need silence. Ahmad has capacity for neither conspiracy or silence. He is like a child who plays about with the stars, arranging them according to his wishes. We laughed at Ahmad when he swore on the heads of all who were present that he would bring Europe to ruin with nothing more than a feather. We laughed and whispered stupid jokes into one another's ears. I remember my friend Muhammad saying to me that night:

"Tell me, is there any space left on this earth for the bodies of all the philosophers and thinkers whom this man has just slain?"

Now I look at his face and recall my loss and my frustration. I feel the need to avenge myself. In spite of the indignation I felt about it, I came to believe that revolution was the act of civilized mankind. And we're only Arabs, who chew qat and smoke hashish – nothing will come from us. Only you can do it. The day that I first slept with you, I did not embrace flesh and blood. You were made of steel, lead and timber. The day we kissed, it was not lips but books and ideologies. I was naïve at the time. I loved books.

"Your health, Ahmad, and here's to everything you'll write about dear Mr Hegel. Tonight we shall toast your victory over Marx."

Ahmad's face betrays his sadness. He puts his glass down and asks:

"How is Frank? Is he still in Paris? I saw that he'd left his wife for you. It's been all over the papers."

Did he want to pay me back for what I had just said? I certainly did not mean to hurt him. Did Ahmad think that when I was attacking all of your gods,that I was attacking him? Hegel, Marx, Nietzsche, all the way down the list of those strange names. Not at all. That wasn't what I meant.

"Ahmad, please don't talk to me about Frank. Why don't we talk about, I don't know, agricultural development in Abu Dhabi?"

Ahmad's face is filled with questions and more questions:

"What's got into you, Nadia? You've changed."

"Oh, Ahmad. Stop it. Look, do you still believe in the possibility of revolution in terrorist countries?"

He tried to keep up with my mania but he was not able to.

"You're acting very strangely this morning, Nadia."

I cry out. My howling voice mixes with the waiter's who has come to collect the bill.

"Ahmad. Do you still believe in the struggle?"

He replies with surprise:

"My convictions have not changed. Death is necessary for us to liberate the . . . "

I watch him spew up the lies of principle and revolution. I look in his face for an edge of truth which I can lean on. There is nothing there. Nothing. I say to him with the self-possession which accompanies the last gasps of a dying man.

"Do you want to know something? I actually killed Frank this morning."

He was amazed that I said it so calmly.

"You killed him! What do you mean you killed him? Are you mad?"

I shall never tell him. What is the difference whether I kill you or whether I bury you alive? There is silence between us. I feel a strange kind of ease. I have freed myself of you. Ahmad takes my hand and leads me to a taxi. He pushes me inside and sits down beside me. He tells the driver our destination. I hear the address of my prison as though for the first time. In the past it was instinct that took me home. It was instinct that made me sleep. I ate, drank, felt affection and made love all as a result of natural impulses. But why is there this sudden return to consciousness in my blood? We both climb the wooden steps. I search for the key. There it is like a child's body in an abandoned tomb. I go in . . . we go in together. He helps me off with my coat and lays me out on the bed.

"Tell me why you killed him."

I find that I am enjoying this play-acting. The text and the stage mingle together. I remain silent. The telephone starts ringing again. It is very loud. Who could be calling at this hour? Ahmad picks up the receiver. It is you, asking whether I am there and if you can have a word with me.

I take your call with the animation of a corpse. Your anger explodes down the line. I let out a hollow laugh. You still know how to get angry then, do you? You want to know why I did what I did. Why did I do it? Why did I tear up your picture. Why did I stab the heart of my poor friend, the old man of the sea? Why did I let my madness erupt in that living-dead flat of yours? Why indeed? It is difficult to explain to you. It's difficult to tell you:

"You. . . ."

But why should I say anything? You don't care enough any more to understand.

"Frank, I'm dying. I have announced it. Please leave me to meet death alone."

We both put down the receiver. I feel the moment of this meeting with death. I look at the face of my friend which was questioning once again. I feel cold. I shiver. It is as if the water is fleeing from my body. I see myself as a water-well becoming limpid in its sorrow. Suddenly I am aware of a noise in the room. It is a strange, unfamiliar sound which comes from behind the radiator. It comes from low down on the wall where I chose to put my distant homeland. Next to the map hang my mother's and father's portraits, along with a couple of pictures of you. I go over towards the radiator, pretending that I am fiddling with its controls. I look behind it and I see a large black insect that is eating into the wall. Questions race into my mind. How long has that been there? How long has it been in my room, eating into my wall? For how long have I been going back into myself?

The wall is old. It is made of old wood. The insect will probably reach the map of my homeland quite quickly. It will probably bring the wall down. I shrug my shoulders and say to myself: It's an old wall; I didn't build it, so who cares?

I head for the kitchen and pour out two whiskies, one for myself and I bring back the other for Ahmad. I sit down on the edge of the bed and raise my glass.

"To you, to the Sa'alik and to vagabonds like us, wherever they may be."

Something greater than fear is trembling inside me. Ahmad knows all about the fleeting moment of lucidity that always comes before the anaesthetic of oblivion. Am I one of those people who is given heightened consciousness by alcohol. Each time I am immersed in a new glass, I awaken for a hundred years while ordinary, stupid, humdrum, daily life is my most powerful narcotic, killing my humanity.

We talk about Lebanon and we get drunk. We talk about Palestine and we get drunk, or rather, we wake up. We talk about plague-ridden revolutions and we are practically slain by the intoxication which that engenders. At no point do I talk about you. You were already buried and I was at peace. I thought that I had finished with you. I believed the moment. I thought that the fleeting moment of joy, which I felt when I climbed out of the well, was something that would last for ever. We continue to drink and slowly the day withdraws from the ashes and from us and from the world. Day is forever treading towards night, never even stopping to tell us where it is going. The noise of the cars reaches us from the Rue Générale Le Clerc and disperses our solitude. We are alone in that moment, with neither a home town nor a homeland, without revolutions or revolutionary examples, without a past, without heroic exploits which we never carried out, or which we carried out only to kill our boredom. I tried to pluck out from inside me, and to throw you at the noise – it's getting louder and louder all the time, coming to me from behind the radiator to conspire against my tranquillity.

Suddenly, I stand up, feeling a bit dizzy after all the Scotch which I have drunk, and I deliver a stirring speech:

"There is no revolution and there are no revolutionaries. There are just ordinary people who live out their lives in silence. It takes courage to live a humdrum life. Take my father, he was a hero to bring nine children into this world and provide for them. Well, he didn't exactly decide to, we came of our own accord. . . . "

Ahmad scoffed at my great discoveries and walked out of my flat.

I locked the door behind him and closed all the windows. I got undressed. I stood naked in front of the mirror and studied my face and body. I was greatly alarmed by the effects of time which could be seen creeping across them. It was worst around my eyes. I heard the sound of the insect mocking me. It seemed to be saying:

"Beautiful lady, you're going to die. You're going to die and you'll never find your homeland."

Screaming wildly I lunged at the mirror and smashed it. I felt like the member of a devastated race . . . the remains of ashes.

The silence carried on howling and the mirror became a thousand mirrors. In the past I used to love mirrors and the peace that those who have given up the struggle make with their souls. In the past I used to feel at ease with the reflection of my face in the mirror. In other people's eyes. In your face. But that moment made me hate myself, and mirrors, and you.

There was a light knock on the door. I leave my life behind me, a hostage to the pieces of glass and the walls and the messages the insect sends me. In a daze, I go over to the door and I open it. You appear before me shrouded in the mists and ashes of oblivion.

"What happened? Why did you do that?"

I do not reply. I head towards my bed and throw my carcass down on it. I hear the voice of Abu Mashour intermingled with yours, and the sound of the insect. My homeland on the wall quivers and you are nailed to the corner. Two conflicting desires pull me. The first one says: You coward! You have run away enough. Where do you think you are going? Do you think that you can escape from your skin? The other voice tells me to stop prevaricating, to go over to you and to bury myself in your arms and try to forget all my heightened consciousness. The revolutionary action which was once so integral to my life, I replaced with you, a revolutionary who has given up the fight.

Ayntab leaves the heart of the Mediterranean and seeks my heart. It kisses me with its lips. It enters into the hollow of my body. It whispers to me: Why are you running from me? Where are you going?

I fear my head is going to explode. The wall shakes. What if the insect arrives at my homeland and devours it . . . I am afraid to run over to the desk and take out the revolver which has been gathering dust in there ever since I was an affectionate lover . . . The revolver which went with me wherever I travelled, like an icon. I had almost forgotten that it was there during my bouts of oblivion. I had almost forgotten the five rounds of ammunition which lay in the chambers, a way for me to find a release. Release from a slow death. I think about opening the drawer but I see your ice-cold hand covering mine. I look at you. You pull me towards the bed and together we set off on another of those journeys of the flesh which take us to oblivion.

When we tried to be together, or rather when I tried to be with you, I forgot everything. In a matter of seconds, I would become like a pussy-cat who nurses its wounds in the heart of the forest. Forgotten is the noise of the insect, forgotten the face of Abu Mashour, forgotten Ahmad and his massacres. Christ has emerged from his sepulchre. He has come down from the Cross. I adorned you with his shroud and we were both lifted to the crest of a tumultuous wave and then hurled down again onto the bed-clothes amid the pleasant moisture of the ocean. I held on to you with all my strength. I felt as though I was clinging to a rock or a tree-root lest I fall into the terrible dark depths of the Ocean. I have forgotten . . . forgotten . . . forgotten.

The night pours into the room. Our bodies are like two corpses spinning through time in search of a sea of tranquillity. My eyes are fixed on the ceiling, I switch on the light. I am surprised when it is your face I see in front of me. I stroke your chest with my hand and say:

"Why did you come?"

You stop me talking by giving me a kiss. Then you ask:

"What's the matter with you? Don't you want to sleep?"

I stay silent. I turn over. Ever since I left my comrades I have been a hostage to sleepless nights. I wake up. I grope my way around the cold, dark streets until tiredness gets the better of me. I come back, exhausted, cram some food into my mouth and then run away to my job. The shafts of light fall on our bodies. My face is turned towards the wall so as not to have to look in your eyes, so as not to have to answer your questions. I am naked. I have forgotten that I should never be completely naked in front of anyone else. That is what the doctor said after he operated on my shoulder to extract the bullet that had been put there by an Israeli agent's gun. Your eyes fall on the place where the bullet went in. I hear both sympathy and surprise in your voice, as you say:

"What's that mark on your right shoulder?"

There is a moment of silence and I think to myself: breathe slowly.

Keep control of yourself. I try to take hold of the net of lies which is my life. The woman-guerrilla, with all her stealth and cunning, is awakened inside me:

"Oh, that. It's nothing. Just an old scar. It's from an operation which I had when I fell off my horse as a girl."

"You used to ride, then?"

My eyes are still facing towards the wall. I am afraid of turning towards you and meeting your gaze. I do not do it because I know that it is not possible for one fighter to conceal his face from another. You cannot cover the mark made by a bullet. Not from a doctor, nor from a fighter. I am sure you did not believe what I said. Not that it mattered . . . At least, that is what I pretended to myself at that moment. I hear you breathing. I feel your breath caressing my shoulder where the bullet went in. I feel the strong desire to cry, or to shout, or to sing, to do anything. I turn around and remember what I was going to say to you.

"Frank, why can't you be more like my homeland?"

You look at me with amazement. Why did I blurt these things out in moments of love and intimacy? Why must I always disturb your state of surrender with pictures of palm-trees and jungles and my homeland?

"Try to sleep, Nadia. Why don't you think of some of the stories your mother used to tell you. You're tired. We need to get out of Paris for a few days. Maybe then you can relax."

It seems that you have not grasped the full extent of my tragedy. It is something that I carry inside me wherever I go. It does not make any difference whether I am in one place or another. I could go and live on a mountain or in a forest. It would always be there. It would always be part of me.

I think of my dear little insect. Yes, it's true. I have grown quite fond of her. She is the only one who calls out to me with complete sincerity.

"Frank, when you were in your cell, did you ever find an insect or something like that?"

You smile and your face is lit up with the past.

"When I was in prison? Oh, I used to think to myself how good the world outside was. I used to have a few ritual pleasures, though. I would think of the beauty of Simone Signoret's eyes. I would dream that . . . "

"Why don't you go back to the Third World, Frank? What is it that keeps you tied to France?"

"Go to sleep. You're very tired . . . France is my country. I have so much to do here."

"You have your comfort and safety here. You've got your beautiful flat in Ile de la Cité. You've got . . . "

You interrupt:

"Everything. That's what is here. My name. My books. The working class whose rights I fight for."

"Oh yes. The right to have a second steak, for instance. The right to have two deserts. Over there they're fighting to stay alive. Why did you come back from the Dark Continent?"

You stay silent. You turn your face to the other wall and go to sleep.

Since that night the insect has accompanied me wherever I go. I try to forget or to escape from it, but in vain. I try to avoid it by doing things which take me out of the house. I go to see my old friends and I tell them about that night. I write. I go to your place. But the insect is always behind me. In front of me. At my side. Everywhere.

I go to my friend al-Bahi and I tell him all about it. We sit down and work out a plan to get rid of it. We go to the Café Saint Claude. We take out sheets of paper. We draft maps of our campaign against the insect. We look at the likelihood of our coming out of the battle victorious. We consider the possibility of failure. We study the feasibility of our moving it to another location. We think what would happen if my army, my whole life in fact, was set free from it. I could send it abroad to one of the embassies where it could represent me, or rather it could represent the Kingdom of the Sa'alik. In the end we can think of no acceptable method. One day, after we had been treated to a rich dinner at Maxime's by one of the 'revolutionary' oil sheikhs, al-Bahi says to me:

"Why don't you just kill it?"

"Are you mad? If I killed it what would I have left? I mean, what could I talk about? At least now it gives me something to chatter on about!"

We agreed that the insect served an important function as a conversation piece, in my heightened consciousness, or rather my intoxication. Then it hits me like a bolt of lightning. A method to rid myself of the insect. I leave al-Bahi and the revolutionary oil sheikh and I go back to my room. I seek it out behind the radiator. There it is, still in its place. I reach down and pick it up. I put it in a small bag. I go to Saint Lazarre Station and get on board a train to Deauville. Down by the water, I lay down on the sand and release the insect so that it can run and jump and play in freedom.

The sun is beating down on me and I close my eyes. When the insect sees what I am doing, it too stretches out and closes its eyes, copying me. After some hours, I open one eye and I see the insect is still lost in its world of dreams. My chance has come and I take it. I run back up to the railway station and I go back to Paris on my own.

Just before I cross the threshold, I stop to listen for a moment. Nothing but the sound of my footsteps on the wooden floor. I look around in my bag for the key. I open the door. A noise from inside hits me like a thunderbolt: the insect is inside the house. It has not moved one inch from its position behind the radiator. I am shivering as I listen to the noise, it mixes with Abu Mashour's voice and my home-land. Once again I see the faces of my comrades. They come to me and torture me in my loneliness. The smell of war and bodies, mutilated by explosives. The face of the River Seine and the prisons of Germany. The smouldering face of Harran. Ayntab asleep. Last of all comes the operation that I took part in there on the Northern Plains. In the depths of the Occupied Land. The action which separated me from my comrades for good.

I returned to Harran via Beirut after I had been forbidden from ever entering West Germany again. I met with a group of comrades in the military wing of the Organization. I was convinced that there was no point in us continuing our external operations and that we should concentrate on hitting at the heart of the Occupied Land. Issam tried to ignore what I was saying. Saleh and Naif also pretended not to hear. Abu Layla said he was tired and so the discussion was adjourned until the following morning.

They thought that I was still suffering the effects of the period I spent in prison. They assumed that I was not in my right mind after my failure and after being wounded during the last hijack. They told me I needed sleep, so I slept. The following day I returned to the subject with a clear head:

"It's no good going back to the old ways. Hijacking planes is getting us nowhere."

The comrades remained entrenched in their positions. I had become a stranger among them. It was the first time that I felt like that in their company. Where was Abu Mashour, so I could tell him about my change of heart and about my coming round to his point of view after all this time?

He was doing active service in one of the encampments on the Northern Plains. He had refused to take part in any more of the external operations. Now he was in charge of our military wing up there.

The comrades had come to their final decision regarding my future among them: I could not possibly take part in any further external operations and, since my face had become known to most of the European intelligence services, I could not participate in any public activity in the camps or in the military wing because I had become, or rather the newspapers had turned me into, some kind of symbolic, bogus heroine. Once again they decided that I should work on the publicity side of the struggle:

"You shall meet the press and do interviews about what you have experienced."

I shouted angrily in Issam's face:

"You're going to make me into a consumer product in other words."

"We are only doing what is required in the interests of the struggle."

"You mean I'm not going to fight again?"

"I'm afraid we can't allow it under present circumstances."

"But I want to join the camps. I still want to do active service."

"That is impossible. You have become a symbol of our struggle and we cannot afford to put your life in danger."

So, while we waited for the media outcry surrounding my release from prison to subside, I stayed in one of the Organization safe houses. I was the recipient of a number of visits from members of our women's section, who kept me informed on the latest developments. At the time the Palestinian struggle was going through one of the most difficult periods of its history. The government in our host country had resolved to finish off our struggle and incidents started to occur in the camps. Things were beginning to take a nasty and bloody turn.

Issam came to the house where I was incarcerated and informed me that the leaders of the Organization had decided that I should take up a position in the information office at Ayntab. I did not answer. I remained silent during his visit. What was there for me to say to him?

The following day I was allowed to leave the house to visit Um Abed. Abu Mashour was with her. When I saw him I ran over to him and flung myself into his arms. He threw me up in the air and started to spin me around like a child. That day, I felt that I was his and that it could never be any other way. He talked to me about everything. I told him of the decision of the leadership regarding my future career as a guerrilla fighter. He told me about the guerrillas who fight in the Northern Plains. He told me of the fantastic morale which they had. I asked whether I could accompany him up there and spend a few days among the fighters – in spite of what my comrades in the military council had said. I was insistent, pleading, and in the end he took me with him.

There I met Farhan once again. Together under the light of an old kerosene lamp, we studied the plans of an operation which was scheduled for the following day. Abu Mashour drew a sketch on paper outlining the military target of the assault; we were to attack the officers' mess in one of the towns close to the border. There was also a political goal, however: to make the other Fedayeen groups recognize our military capability and to allow representatives of our organization to attend the meeting of the Palestinian National Council which was shortly to take place in Cairo. All night we studied the plans, considering every possible eventuality. It occurred to me that the reconnaissance side of the operation had not been satisfactorily completed and that there were grounds for a postponement to make sure that we were not being exposed to any unnecessary military risks, particularly since the moon was full and even the tiniest pebble would be fully illuminated at this time of the month. Farhan was against the postponement because it would mean missing the opportunity to impose ourselves on the National Council. Two hours later we received a call from the command in Harran requesting that we carry out the orders immediately because of the early commencement of the Cairo talks with the vote being taken on the following day.

Abu Mashour divided us into four groups and assigned a specific area to each group. The first was made up of fifteen men who would cross into enemy territory and attack the officers' mess, while a second group of fifteen would be in position on the Tarshiha side in a supporting role. A third group of ten fighters was to be stationed in the village of al-Mansoura, to create a diversion for a squadron of enemy tanks stationed in the area. That left ten fighters who were to remain in the camp. I was told to stay at the rear with the fourth group. I was instructed to look after a French journalist who was doing a story on the Palestinian resistance forces for a leftist French newspaper. We were to link up with the first group on their return from the occupied area, giving medical treatment to any wounded men and passing on any intelligence that we might have gathered during the operation and finally escorting the assault team back to base.

The distribution of fighters among the various groups looked wrong to me. I told Abu Mashour that it was an unnecessary risk to have so many of our people in the village all at the same time. I also suggested that he did not put himself at the head of the operation. After Geneva, I knew that if there was one problem with Abu Mashour, it was that he was too courageous, and that he took too many risks. In urban guerrilla fighting, courage like that was something of a liability, and he would be a danger both to himself and to his comrades. But Abu Mashour felt that I was casting aspersions on his capabilities as a commander, and the harder I tried to convince him to pass the command to Farhan, and take charge of the al-Mansoura team, the more insistent he was upon leading the main assault group. I thought that at least he could count on the assistance of the Arab inhabitants of al-Mansoura if the incursion was not successful, but my arguments were wasted on them. They would not even agree to a postponement until such time as the issues of the reconnaissance and the redistribution could be resolved. It was decided that the teams should set off for their targets at midnight.

I stood in front of the building which we were occupying and said goodbye to each of the fighters as they set off. I joked with one of them, whom we called Ali 'Carlo' after his favourite weapon, that I would not let him back in the camp unless he brought back a basket of the famous al-Mansoura apples. Abu Mashour came up to me and kissed me on each cheek without saying a word . . . no final requests.

How futile our words are! All the words in the world could not convey what was in my heart at that moment. They went off into the dark. As the senior member of my team, I started organizing the men in their reconnaissance duties. Then the journalist asked me to give him an interview for his paper, but I told him it was out of the question. An hour later we could see that some of the tanks were moving through the village of al-Mansoura towards the higher ground. This meant that our comrades would not be able to strike at the main target. I had to warn them immediately. I took hold of the wireless set and tried to contact the advance assault team. I heard my voice saying over and over again:

"Come in, Abu Mashour. Come in, Abu Mashour. Enemy tanks approaching from the south. You must pull back. You must pull back."

My voice was drowned by the sound of shelling. Explosions. Tracer bombs and flares lit up the whole area. I could see Arum everywhere, dressed up in her June livery, her face coming out at me from every corner. I threw myself onto my stomach near one of the walls and shouted to my comrades not to open fire so as not to give our position away. The Frenchman gazed at me with surprise and admiration as he scribbled notes. I shouted at him to get down. A flare crossed above the roof of the house and I felt the foundations being shaken. I could get no answer to the radio warning I sent. With bitterness I realized that my comrades were probably under a heavy attack and could not use the wireless. I decided that our group should head towards the target to try to reach them. I went out into the courtyard and summoned everyone to me. When they were all present we set off with our small arms. The French journalist came with us. The building behind us was plunged into darkness. A shell exploded close by. Everything turned to fire. I advanced a further ten yards when another mortar passed very close to our position. I leapt away in an attempt to get away from the explosion. One of my comrades was hit. I saw him being thrown to the ground, his face covered in blood. I shouted to everyone to get down, and we waited for the battle to subside a little before we moved off again. At that moment I heard the regular Arab artillery returning fire and we decided to pull back to our original position. I realized that to advance in such difficult circumstances was impossible. It seemed that the enemy already knew our position because their fire was landing frighteningly close to us. We picked up our casualty, who was still alive, and what weapons and ammunition we could salvage and retreated to a dug-out to the rear of our base.

All through the night the artillery fire continued to pass over our heads and it only quietened down with the first threads of daylight. I tried to contact the assault group once more from the dug-out. This time I heard Farhan's voice saying:

"Try to save the comrades. We were ambushed."

The blood pounded in my head. I was incapable of doing anything. I asked more questions about the ambush, but the signal had gone and the only sound was my voice repeating anxiously:

"Hello . . . Farhan . . . Come in. Are you able to retreat? Hello."

The morning sun fell on our dug-out. We heard voices approaching us. I put the wireless aside and I picked up my rifle. Over the edge of the dug-out I could see the al-Mansoura team returning. They were carrying two wounded men. The artillery from the enemy side had fallen silent. I ran out to help the wounded comrades into the building and there, with the help of the French journalist, I dressed their wounds. Their silent faces looked like wax, as if death itself had taken over their features. We all knew that Abu Mashour's party would not be returning. I felt a searing pain. Never again was I to see his face. Never again would I see the faces of Ali Carlo or Farhan. But I could not let myself be overcome by these thoughts. I had an important task to carry out. I had to relocate our base as soon as possible. Not only did the enemy know of our position but the fact that fifteen of our comrades had fallen into their hands made matters considerably worse. We did not know what the circumstances were under which they succumbed. Would they hold out under interrogation or would they confess?

I gave the order for us to begin moving our weapons and vehicles. We all helped load things onto the trucks and when we had finished we headed towards the interior. On our way back to the south-east we were stopped by a regular army patrol who asked us to accompany them to a nearby army encampment. I tried to draw the patrol leader on what the reasons were for our being detained, assuring him that there was no need for it. It transpired that our incursion had been made without permission, in other words without getting prior permission from the Ministry of Defence. This was a bone of contention between the regular army and the guerrilla fighters. What we were meant to do, according to the agreements made between the Palestinians and the government, was to submit out request for permission to carry out a military operation a fortnight in advance of the date of the action. Previously, this had caused our organization all kinds of difficulties because the enemy positions which we needed to target would be there one day and gone the next. Therefore, our comrade leaders in the north had been forced to launch a number of attacks without having obtained the correct permission. Those attacks had been on a small scale and could be overlooked, but the previous night's operation had resulted in the intervention of the regular army, and that broke the cease-fire agreement which followed the Fifth of June hostilities.

We went into one of the regular army camps where we were met by a Lieutenant-Colonel who asked us to get down from the vehicle and go into one of the tents. Then he requested that the head of the operation come for a talk with him in his tent. As the most senior person left in the group I followed him into his tent. When he realized who I was he jumped to his feet and stared at me with astonishment.

"You!"

He must have seen my picture in the papers in the wake of the last operation that I had carried out in Germany. I had been all over the press after that. Every front page had carried my picture, calling me 'the courageous leopardess', 'a legend', 'a star', 'fanatical female terrorist', and so on. Abu Mashour had been right when he told me that day in Geneva that heroism was a matter of daily life for those comrades who fight and die in silence. I could feel that the officer was hesitating, so I took the lead:

"We are grateful for your support in yesterday's operation."

He said nothing, so I went on:

"We regret that we did not have the opportunity to wait for permission from the Ministry. Our reconnaissance showed that the target was on the move."

Again he remained silent.

"It is hoped that we will be able to relocate our base, given that a number of our comrades fell into enemy hands. There is a very real danger to us if we remain where we are at the moment."

He shook his head silently and tapped his foot on the ground. Finally he spoke:

"As you well know, there is great danger attached to any incursion made without notifying us and waiting for a report based on our studies of the conditions of the area. It's for your own safety. You must realize that there are no other circumstances in which the Ministry would withhold its permission."

With that, the official voice of authority fell silent. It reminded me of June in Arum when the town was just about to fall to the enemy. That day I kissed hands. I begged and pleaded to each and every one of them to give me anything to defend myself with, even if it was only a knife. They refused. I didn't know what to say to them at the time. My comrades' blood was seeping into the earth on the hill which we had abandoned. I just wanted to know what our position was. I put my questions as directly as I could . . . whether or not we could relocate our base; whether or not we could go to Harran to tell our leaders what had happened. After an hour of negotiations, he decided to contact his superiors and await their answer.

Slow hours passed while we waited. My comrades sat around as the sun climbed up the sky and sent its powerful rays down onto our bodies. I turned to one side and moved the needle of the wireless to one of the enemy stations to pick up the midday news broadcast. My suspicions, that Abu Mashour's team had been discovered before they got anywhere near their target, were confirmed; the broadcast reported that the fighting had resulted in the capture of all guerrillas apart from the three who had been killed.

The news went on to say that there was confirmation of the presence of saboteurs camped near to al-Mansoura. That meant that our comrades had confessed, but we still didn't know which ones, or under what circumstances. The enemy station did not disclose the names of those who had died, nor did they give any clue as to their identities. This made me suspect that Farhan and Abu Mashour were still alive. If they were among the dead then surely the enemy radio would have announced the fact, to demonstrate their success over the local leaders of our organization. But then again, perhaps the comrades who survived the ambush had not told their captors the names and positions of those who had fallen. So nothing was certain in the matter.

At noon a private soldier came into the tent which I had been assigned and told me that I was requested to appear for an interview with the section commander. I went in to his tent and found him sipping a cup of coffee. He stood up when I entered and held out his hand to shake mine. He then courteously informed me that his superiors had given their consent to our relocation on the condition that I, on behalf of the leadership of my organization, give an undertaking that no further operations would be initiated without prior agreement with the Ministry.

"As you know, operations like this bring us into confrontation which we are still not prepared for."

He said this as he was handing over his commanders' written consent. I thanked him and was just about to leave the tent when he said:

"And if I was your superior, I'd be a bit more careful about where I put someone like you. You're a symbol now and they should never have let you come as close to death as you did last night."

Once again I saw the image Abu Mashour and I felt reassured by the simplicity and sincerity of his feelings. I smiled submissively to the officer and left the tent.

When I got back to my comrades, I could see the tiredness on their faces, in their eyes, in the hang of their limbs. I told them that the commanders of the regular army had agreed we could relocate our position. Everyone was happy as we left the compound. We said goodbye to the soldiers and thanked them for giving us something to eat and drink. We had spent some time with them discussing our conviction that all the Arabs should be involved in the struggle against Israel. We headed for Harran. I had to submit a detailed report about what happened in the Northern Plains, since it was a matter of considerable importance. The loss of two of our best fighters, both of whom were members of the military command of our organization, put us in a critical position in that period of the struggle.

I was an island of sorrow during our journey back to Harran. It was under twenty-four hours since I had lost my friend, but I had no right to grieve for him. People like us are not allowed the luxury of grief. I couldn't imagine Abu Mashour's face in that hour when he fell into their hands. I could not understand what he was saying when he left me:

"The struggle is more complicated than we think."

Did he know that he was not coming back? Did he really risk his life, and the lives of his comrades, for an operation with such dubious goals. If that was the case then we had to look at matters in a different way. We could not be sympathetic.

All of these questions, Frank, inhabited my head and I could not find any answers. It is getting near the end of the night. I love Abu Mashour and I wait for his return.

That evening in Harran, I went to see the military council to discuss what had happened. In the opinion of a majority of the comrades, it was I who was to blame for the losses. After listening to my special report on the operation, Naif requested that I be put on trial.

The two things which stood against me were: travelling to the north without permission of the leadership, which contravened their resolution that I should not return to any of the bases, and not notifying the leadership of the result of the operation until the following day.

Of all of my accusers at the meeting, Issam was the most virulent in his attacks on me. He spat out his words:

"This is not a poetry circle, Nadia, this is a resistance movement. Orders must be obeyed. You can't go around following your emotions like this."

My reply to Issam was equally sharp. I reminded him what it was like before the Fifth of June. I reminded him of the hard days. I reminded them of the mistakes which we all made and which could have led us to destruction. "I am no saint. I admit that I have made mistakes but I was afraid of never again being given the opportunity to take up arms in our struggle."

We moved to the second of their accusations against me and I argued with them about the planning of the operation and the results of the reconnaissance missions which the comrades had undertaken before its execution. I told them that I had never been completely happy about the conditions and I told them that there was not sufficient reconnaissance carried out before embarking on an operation which was to employ all of our military might in the area.

My observations were not received well. Saleh's expression showed unease. I heard Naif saying:

"The operation had to take place before the convening of the National Council. It was the only way for us to be adopted as one of the Palestinian resistance groups."

I threw in my hand. Faces and voices merged together for an instant . . . It seemed to me as though Naif's face had been transformed into an elaborate mask. You could have made up a thousand copies of it and given one to each of the Arab rulers to wear at official celebrations and feast days. What is the difference between us and our leaders? The small fry are sacrificed so that the big fish can get what they want. Sending fifteen men to their deaths at a single throw, just to get a few votes at the National Council . . . Surely that was a crime. Oh no, it was justifiable in the name of tactics and strategy. The result is just the same though, isn't it.

They came to their decision. I was to go back to Ayntab to work in one of their bureaux as a publicity officer. That, and ten days imprisonment for disobeying orders and going to a military base without their permission.

I went into detention the following day. I was put in a small room filled with books in one of the camps in Wadi Musa. I had been received by a guerrilla fighter who put me in the cell. He laughed as he closed the door behind me, saying:

"Comrade Nadia, you just need to be patient, and you can pass the time reading up on your Marxist theories."

I did not take it too badly, but I was sorry that I was going to be moved far away from the encampments and my comrades-at-arms. I realised that they had again decided to plant me into the dead, post-Fifth of June streets of the Arab cities. Turned into a cheap product for consumption by journalists and newspapers. I was to return to the coffee-house intellectuals of Ayntab, whom I had left behind and forgotten about during my years of action.

During those ten days, I had time to ponder the death of Abu Mashour. Had he in fact escaped death and was now being held in captivity? I felt the pain reach my innermost being. He was one of the best of us, and his death would be a great loss to our military organization.

His face came to me, engraved on the pages of the books, traced in the face of my guards, drawn on the window which brought in the few rays of sunlight to my cell. I realized that I loved him. I thought back to the days in Geneva when we were two bodies in a bed, with the snow covering the lake outside. I remembered his uncertainty about whether our external operations served any useful purpose. I remembered his face in the aeroplane when he whispered in my ear:

"If we get out of this alive, I'll always love you, you know."

I remembered when we parted on the night of the operation, and the way he kissed me on the forehead. Oh God, how hard it is to be in love with a fighter.

During my imprisonment, I read a lot and slept a little. I read Che Guevara's memoirs of the war in Cuba. I was particularly interested in passages which dealt with the revolutionaries' relationship with the inhabitants of Sierra Maestra. It was that relationship which helped them to see their struggle through to its conclusion. It made me think how weak our links were with the ordinary Palestinians up until now. We had always behaved towards them in the same way that we had behaved towards the media, telling them exaggerated stories of our military might and our capabilities. It occurred to me that working with the media might give me an opportunity to change this situation.

Paris 1977.

The walls of my room. My wall. The one with the map of my homeland. The pictures of my mother and father. You. The picture of Abu Mashour stored in my memory. All my comrades. The wall is shaking. I get a migraine at this hour. I can hear the buzzing of the insect. I am a prisoner of my papers and my desire to escape to a place far away from all this, a place where there are no insects and no homelands and no memories.

I am torn apart by sounds and memories. The wind outside torments me. Frank, where are you? Do you remember how crazy I was? Do you remember how I used to try to escape from all of this. I used to seek refuge in you and look for a little sympathy and tenderness from you.

I came to you once, at the end of the night, dragging my limbs. Escaping from the insect. Escaping from myself. I climbed the seven flights of stairs to your flat. I stood before the wooden door, panting and pretending not to notice the sounds of the mice and the dogs in the well-heated apartments. I knocked firmly on your door and you opened it. When you see my face in the corridor, you hold out your arms to guide me over the threshold. There is a look of surprise on your face as you say to me:

"What brings you here? Happiness or depression?"

I come in and head straight to the sofa opposite your desk. I always liked to throw myself down on that one. The moments pass as you are looking at me, the corpse of your memories spread out in the papers lying on your desk. I ask you:

"Are you still writing?"

"The novel is finished and I've got to send it to the publishers this month."

"What is it about? Revolution. The armed struggle. Guerrilla fighters."

"And you."

I was surprised.

"Me! Why should it be about me?"

"Why? Oh, I don't know. I tried to bring you and them together."

"Do you still think about your old comrades? I would have thought the distance between you has grown too great."

"Yes. I think about them, and I write about them. I don't have a choice, really. They are there in my head."

"Why don't you go back to them?"

"I can't. There is no place for me there. I'm here, in my own country, where no one asks me where I've come from. Only the most curious person wants to know my family name and the town where I was born."

"Dear Frank. You've even abandoned your role as an expert adviser, haven't you?"

A moment of silence passes over us. We both fight it so that we can carry on our journeys of oblivion. How we need legends, Frank. That moment really made me feel how squalid our lives are . . . I feel that our bodies do not have the right to carry our heads . . . I didn't need to ask you what your novel is about. I know perfectly well what goes on inside your head. We both escape to love . . . We both flee to our bodies, as we always do. Two rotting corpses, no more, no less.

It is raining outside . . . It is raining and I am an island of oblivion. I shiver out on the pavement, refusing to go back inside the four walls.

The insect is in my house. The insect accompanies me wherever I go. My body is wracked by torment when I hear its song. I flee . . . I flee. I seek refuge with my friend the Ambassador of Hate who comes from the land of sleep and warmth. I try to talk to him about it . . . about you . . . about God. But he too is escaping, escaping from me to God and his two wives and his tribe of children. Together we practise the game of fleeing to other things and other worlds.

The night passed. Paris breathes slowly before the mornings of chill and love, as if announcing its boredom of the world. It was black. Like my face. In the evening, our story enters its second year and the insect has been with me for some months now. How I hoped to return to my house and find that the buzzing had stopped, that my insect had been struck dumb, had lost its memory, had died . . . Oh, if only it were dead! Why did you leave me alone in Paris, Frank? Why did you go away?

Frank, I am afraid. . . .

Before you, I was obsessed by being an exile. I forgot my comrades, or at least I pretended to forget them. Before you, I would refuse to meet them in Paris. I fled from any situation where I might hear news about them. I tried to reconcile myself to things and time and to accept an ordinary woman's life. That was before you . . . let us stop here. That is enough. I want to start again.

I was a wife. That is how I remember it now. It happened without any warning on my return from Harran to Ayntab. One of my comrades told me:

"You had better have plastic surgery on your face. It is too well known now, and Ayntab is a town open to the sea. It's full of tourists and drug runners and it would be very difficult for us to keep an eye on you all the time."

I had become a burden on my comrades! I went with one of my doctor comrades to this clinic. It was the clinic of my husband-to-be. He was a very famous cosmetic surgeon. We spoke to him about my desire to have plastic surgery, explaining to him the difficulties of my carrying on with the way I looked at the time. (I couldn't even keep my face!)

I remember him now with some tenderness.

He was in his forties, and he came from an old family in the south, which had a long tradition of supporting Arab nationalist causes. He returned to his country after he had spent ten years completing his studies in Europe. He tried to plant himself in the earth of his homeland once again, but he found that he did not have any roots there. Then one day I walked into his clinic, (still suffering the effects of the mental breakdown which had struck me during the last days of my imprisonment). I looked haggard, skinny and anxious. When I lay down on the couch opposite his desk I told him that what was to pass between us would have to remain completely secret. He got up from his desk and came round to the couch. He put his finger on my lips as if to silence me.

"I have heard a lot about you, but I did not know that you were still fighting. You needn't worry. It'll all be over quickly."

I smiled.

"I've heard a lot about you too. But I didn't know that you were still so young!"

He laughed and went out of the room. When he came back a few minutes later, he was carrying a pile of photographs of different kinds of noses. There were long noses and short noses, sharp ones, small ones, noses which seemed to rest in the middle of faces with perfect joy and happiness. There were even oblong noses.

"Pick a nose," he said.

I laughed at the idea.

"I am going to get a new nose?"

"What did you think I was going to do? We can't change anything else on your face."

"Will I still be able to smell the scent of jasmine? Or gunpowder, or the stench of Arab politics?"

This time he laughed.

"Well, I can't make any promises about the jasmine, but I can guarantee the second and third things. Especially the third."

He held on to my hand, and noticed that it was trembling slightly. For all my joking, the idea of changing my nose troubled me. He said to me:

"Don't worry. We have already seen how brave you can be. It'll all be over very quickly."

He led me to the operating theatre and I saw the rows of scalpels and scissors, bandages and ligatures. He had me stretch out on the operating table under the many lights which were trained on my face. We waited for one of the comrade doctors to arrive to administer the anaesthetic.

In the moments before the operation, I felt a longing to be able to belong to something other than death and secret political movements. And there was his face bringing light into the room. His calmness imparted to me a need to belong. To belong temporarily to a different tempest. To travel on a different train. To smell the wild perfume of primeval forests. It was indeed all over very quickly. I do not know how he knew, but the doctor told me afterwards that he felt I was happy to be rid of that nose which had been blocked up by war and the stench of dead bodies and Arab politicians.

I woke up to a terrible pain in the middle of my face. All my nerves seemed to be centred on that one place. I tried not to cry out or to complain. He came to me that evening and gave me a pain-killing injection and told me to get some sleep. Before he left me, he sat on the side of the bed and told me how brave I had been during the operation.

I heard my laugh echoing back to me against the white walls. What did he mean by 'brave'? What is gone is gone. What has passed has passed. June '67 made me an island of endurance. It made me realise that war is not only a knife but also the ability to endure.

My days in the hospital passed and his face did not leave me. He would come in the morning to change my bandages. He would return in the evening and talk to me about what he had done during the day.

One day, when I had got back some of my vitality, he took my hand and sat on the edge of the bed.

"Tell me about your life. I read in the papers that you used to be a poet. Do you write any poetry nowadays?"

His question took me back to a world which I had almost forgotten. Poetry. Yes, I used to write poetry, before I joined their ranks.

I replied:

"I have abandoned poetry. I am now trying to live it among my comrades."

He did not seem convinced. He carried on stroking the back of my hand. I gave myself up to this new and pleasurable feeling, like an intoxicated traveller carried away on the crest of a wave.

"They say that you are not of Arab descent. Is that true?"

I nodded my head. It seems that I will never be free of my blood affiliations.

"I'm Kurdish, originally. That is, on my father's side"

"So how come you took up arms with *them*? I mean . . . "

His question took me back to my childhood. The day I first found out that I was from a nation other than the one for which I was fighting. I remembered my grandmother and her strange, unfamiliar language. The way my father mocked me when I joined one of the most hard-line Arab Nationalist groups. I thought back to the first time that I heard the poems of Sulaiman Issa. I shook my head and replied:

"What difference does it make whether I am an Arab or a Kurd? I have always lived among the Arabs and have always been with their cause. Arabic language . . . Arab history . . . Arab faces accompanying me through my childhood."

The conversation moved on.

"They say that you are a Kurdish princess. Is that true?"

I smile. The myths come out again!

"A princess? I don't know . . . my father was the one who took care of our family tree. You'd better ask him about that . . . To me that sort of thing is about as interesting as the population figures of Djakarta."

My days in the hospital made me feel a closeness with that calm, self-assured face . . . His company during the hours which he had off from his clinic made me feel an emotion which was something like the desire for life itself. I had known death, and now I desired life, and he came to me carrying life in his hands. A few days after I left the hospital, Khalid and I got married and I moved to live with him in one of the villas close to the entrance to Ayntab.

That day, the comrades discussed the reasons for my marriage and came to the conclusion that I was escaping from the difficulties which we were faced with on the Ayntab front. I tried not to let my marriage get in the way of my duties. I used to spend the whole day in one of the refugee camps, keeping up with the news, receiving cyphers and letters, re-drafting political reports which I would send to the leadership in Harran, receiving reports and foreign visitors, taking visitors around the military encampments. In the evenings I would go back to my home where I would play my wifely role with calm and composure. A woman

. . . a woman cooking meals for her family and fretting over the minor details of life. We would sit together in the evening, reading and listening to Wagner. I was a great lover of Wagner. I did not feel that there was any inconsistency in my life . . . I played my role calmly and confidently. I don't know where these qualities came from, but I seemed to have acquired them in the whirlwind of anxiety which lives in the field of battle.

For the first time, after an absence of two years from my family, my mother came to Ayntab and settled down with me in the big house, a few days later my father followed. I was deliriously happy to see them again. After a year and a half of living the life of a fugitive, I was able to enjoy the pleasures of family life once more.

"Did you love your husband?"

"I was with him, but I was waiting for Abu Mashour."

You look at my face in surprise and ask me:

"Who is this Abu Mashour?"

I remember that it is not right for me to talk about him:

"Oh, just an old friend."

"Why did you get married then?"

"Please, no more questions. Just leave me in peace."

He tried very hard to get me to lead a more 'normal' life – that's what he used to call it. A normal life for him meant the house, dinner parties, invitations, holidays. He couldn't see that that sort of thing was not normal for me any more. In spite of this, the first few months passed without any big problems or disagreements.

One day I was on my way back home from my office at the camp, when I suddenly felt dizzy. It made me think that my period was five days late that month. He was by my side but I did not tell him because I knew how much he wanted to have a child. As far as I was concerned the time had not yet come for me to take a decision of that kind.

In the evening, I told my mother the news and real joy appeared on her face. She said to me:

"You must have the baby. Don't forget that you are twenty-eight now and your husband is in his forties."

I remained silent. This was something I had to think about. What did it mean for me to be a mother? Could I give him a child while living this life of mine?

After a long period of hesitation, I told him and he reacted with love and enthusiasm. When the news had sunk in, he paused for a moment and asked me to lighten my workload at the Organization's information office and to give myself a little time to relax.

I was taken completely by surprise. Everything that I had forgotten in my life, was brought back to me then. Did I have to change my life and become an expectant mother? What about my work in the Organization? What about my role as a fighter and the part I played in the lives of my comrades? Wasn't that enough to make me a woman?

A few days later, Khalid, who had never come to see me at work before, visited me at my office. He found me among the piles of papers and stencilling machines, the ink and the noise from the radio receivers. He asked me whether I could take a break from work and cut down the two hours of military training which I took every day. The training was because I didn't want to allow myself to get rusty. A guerrilla fighter – and you know this as well as anyone, Frank – is like his weapon. If either of them is allowed to fall into misuse, the rust sets in quickly and the mechanism is ruined. My feelings of failure, frustration and confusion overtake me. My husband's face looks like the face of a stranger to me. Oh God. What made me want to put myself into the lottery of everyday life?

I am not my own woman any more!

This expression echoed in my head and I stared hard into his face. For the first time I experienced alienation from my husband. Like strangers on a train – the first stop and we shall part.

Before him, in other words before marriage, home and pregnancy, I thought that coming home at night to a man would restore my equilibrium and would enable me to follow my path with greater clarity and certainty.

Before this my life had been a wonderful, if taxing, adventure. It never occurred to me, as I was searching for revolution in the airports of Europe, that the day would come when I had to choose between my natural, 'normal' role and my real life. Little by little, I gave in to an easier way of living. I tried to shorten the hours which I spent training, limiting myself to one hour a day. Soon I was down to half an hour a day, but then came Black September.

The battle flared up suddenly in Harran. On the Northern Plains.

In all the fields of combat which I had abandoned. One by one, my comrades started to arrive in Ayntab. The Arab cities were in flames.

My workload at the information bureau increased and events began to follow one another with alarming speed. I had to cut myself off from home so that I could devote myself to work in the bureau. I slept there and wrote my papers there. I kept an eye on the news and the foreign agency news wires. I also studied the few reports which were issued by the Leadership. As usual they told us about the valour of our fighters and what a strong position we were in. As the days went by, their bodies were piling up on the roadsides of Harran, and the world looked on without saying a word. I completely forgot about the embryo which was growing in my womb. I forgot that I was a wife, with a house and a husband and a family. I forgot that I belonged to the normal, everyday life of the Ayntab streets. I lived in my office and doubled the hours of my military training. I was terrified by the prospect of sparks from Harran igniting a conflict in Ayntab. A miasma of killing and expulsion. The contagion of silence about everything that came to pass.

Khalid would ring me up every morning and ask me whether I was going to have supper at home with him in the evening. Home! How could he talk about home amidst all this killing and blood-letting?

No love. No husband. The knife which was June became the bullets and bombs of September. It was no longer possible to remain silent. Life was not possible any more. International reports and official institutions cry out all their vapidities when faced with innocent children who have been caught in the flames.

Things happened quickly. Harran was surrounded. The encampments to the north were surrounded. The comrades were run to ground. The smell of corpses came to me on the breeze and in the words of those who had fled. The battle survivors returned to us bearing their wounds and their failure, and went into hiding. All the time I was waiting for the miracle which would deliver those who were still out there. But my hopes were drowned in blood and I had to come to terms with the harshness of living in our age.

After a fortnight of the battle, I received a telex from the Leadership requesting that I begin preparations to receive and provide shelter for some members of the political bureau who were planning to retreat to Ayntab. This was a most difficult request because the host country was already having grave doubts about our presence. A few days earlier the matter had been discussed in the parliament. In the evening I telephoned my father-in-law who was still in the south and requested his help in finding hide-outs for the comrades. He hesitated for a long time before suggesting that they be moved to one of the villages in the south, close to the border, where they could be looked after in case of an outbreak of hostilities in Ayntab. I agreed with the idea and went off in my car to a place near the battle zone. I waited for them to arrive. After an hour, Saleh and Muhammad appeared, but Issam was not with them. I started the car and we set off towards Ayntab. My hands were trembling on the steering-wheel as we crossed the Beka'a Valley. I looked at their tired faces and their straggly beards.

I could smell the sweat on their bodies along with cordite and earth. I remembered with grief and despondency that I was planning to become a mother, to have a child in this world of killing and expulsion and homelessness. It now seemed like madness to be bringing another refugee into the Arab world. Suddenly I did not want that foetus in my body any more, dishonouring my womb. I had to be free of it. Trying to fulfil my natural role in this atmosphere was absurd. How could I be an honest and effective mother now? How could I meekly bridge the gap between my husband and his sons and never speak about why I chose that shameful moment to conceive a child?

I had not had any contact with them since that day when I left them in Harran, but Saleh knew everything:

"How is married life? We heard you are pregnant. We'll all be so pleased when you have the baby."

A wave of profound shame swept over me when I thought of Saleh bidding farewell to his children in Palestine, never to set eyes on them again. I made a great effort to appear natural and calm without letting them realise the pit of despair that I was in and the contradiction that I was living. I wanted to dispel this loathsome moment, so I turned to Saleh and said:

"Yes, I have agreed to become a mother, finally."

The route to Ayntab was winding and passed through the mountains. My hands clung to the wheel. My face was submerged in the gloom of the future. What did the future hold for me?

In the light of the street lamps, I saw a swelling around Saleh's right eye. I stopped the car and turned in my seat to look at the wound, the blue ring around his eye.

I reached out my hand and touched the blue ring around his eye. I asked him if he wanted me to take him to my house where my husband could make a quick examination of the wound. It was only then that I saw that Muhammad had lost an arm and had been hiding it from me by putting his combat jacket over his shoulder. The two comrades saw my shock and bravely tried to lessen the impact by joking with me:

"Nadia, you're looking older. Don't tell me that married life doesn't agree with you!"

I could not cope with their light-heartedness. What could I say? I looked to my courage to save me. I tried to grant myself life and I remembered that no one can have life if they do not ultimately accept death. Death had ceased to frighten me and I considered it an ordinary matter which could spring up on you at any time. A car crash. Crossing the road. A stray bullet. There was no doubt that the battle was going to be long and I still had a lot of time.

When we arrived in Ayntab, I took them straight home, passing through the district of well-heated villas, their lights beaming out into the dark. I thought about the criminals and murderers who inhabited these buildings, their whisky and their perfumes, their rich pickings from the crumbs under oil-rich tables in Arabia. At my side were the faces of the real fighters, those who had chosen repudiation and death in order to gain life. I stopped in front of our house and got out of the car. We crossed the garden to the front door. My feet felt as though they could hardly support my body. Khalid saw me from the window and hurried down to meet me. He took me in his arms and I put my head on his shoulder.

I wanted to cry. I was home after fifteen days away, fifteen days since the fighting broke out in Harran.

We went through to the hall which my husband had furnished in the most beautiful and luxurious fashion. But everything appeared to be trivial and beneath contempt. The richness looked more like putrefaction. I looked at their faces. That was where my homeland was. Why should I look elsewhere? I did not dare ask them how many fighters we had lost. I felt that they were hiding something from me. I did not ask them about Issam and Naif. I had read in the newspaper that they were surrounded in a house in Harran three days before and that they were still fighting.

We were as silent as corpses in the grave. Khalid was looking at me before turning to my comrades. My mother came in with coffee for everyone. I got up to help her. She kissed me and then burst into tears.

"It's alright, I'm here. Why are you crying? What's the matter?"

She left me and went back to her bedroom. Silence descended on the four of us.

At the dinner table Saleh told me about the fierce fighting in Harran. Then he paused for a moment before telling me that Um Abed was also among the dead. She had been gunned down outside the Organization headquarters. I stopped eating and looked at his face icily. I saw her in front of me, her round face and full figure. I could hear her loud voice telling me about their flight from Jerusalem and her dream of reunifying Palestine. Had all that really finished? I remembered her valour and her simplicity. I fought back the tears. I arranged to meet the comrades the following day and they left. I found myself alone to face my husband and my parents. I found myself submitting to 'normal', daily life once more, in the realms of luxury and ease. They did not ask me anything. They remained silent. I looked at each of them and prayed that someone would say something, anything. I addressed my husband:

"Khalid, was it wrong for me to bring them here?"

He said nothing.

"Why don't you answer? Did you know that Issam and Naif are still cut off?"

Again, nothing.

"Why don't you say something?"

He held out his hand and helped me to my feet. He led me to the bedroom.

For the first time in a fortnight, I felt clean sheets against my skin and a sense of comfort. I tried to explain to my husband how important it was for me to support my comrades in Harran, how I wanted to stop the bullets from tearing into their bodies. My husband did not speak. I felt that the walls of alienation, which I had lived with all my life, were now being raised between us. There was no longer any point in us living the moments when things were falling apart. I decided to discuss our future together. But then I felt a pain in my stomach and a burning sensation in my head. I tried to fight against it but it was too great. I had been unaware of how my body had swollen over the last days. Seconds passed and suddenly everything was bathed in blood. I passed out.

I spent three days lying in a bed in the American University Hospital wrestling with life and death after the doctors had aborted the foetus that was inside me. There was nothing they could do. It had been dead for days.

When I opened my eyes there was his face. And the faces of my parents. I could not cry. I could not feel any pain. Joy had left my body. The past was the present in my memory, while the future slept under a curtain of fear and the expectation of death.

I stayed in hospital for ten days, before going back home in a state of utter dejection. I threw myself into the bed of peace and wealth like an old rag, trying to bring back the memory of those last days in the refugee camp. I felt an enigmatic, temporary, peace, like the calm which inhabits the souls of those condemned to be hanged in a few short minutes. No doubt there are many victims stretched out on the pavements of Harran, some of them still suffering, the spirit not yet having left the body. There were no ambulances, no doctors, no clean hospital beds. How had Um Abed met her death? Was she killed outright in a hail of bullets? Or had she lain wounded for days before drawing her last breath? Had anyone been able to get close to her or had they not dared to risk the snipers' bullets? Had Naif managed to escape, or was he still imprisoned there? There were no answers to my questions so I would get out of bed and wander through the rooms searching for my mother. When I found her in the sitting-room with her eyes fixed on the heavens, I would put my head on her breast and sob like a child. I would then get up again and go from room to room in a state of bewilderment. I saw the eyes of children in the walls. They were being suffocated in a shower of burning ashes. I heard their anguished cries as they pleaded for help. Sometimes I would run over to the wall and hold out my hand to touch them. But only cold plaster met my fingers. As my daily journeys around the house got more frequent, my mother's concerns about my sanity increased. She told my husband about my condition. One evening he came to me with some books and a bunch of flowers which he put into a vase in my room. I do not know why but the books turned into corpses in my hands and their putrefying stench stuck in my nostrils so that I could no longer draw breath.

I was scared. In an attempt to defend myself I shouted in his face:

"Get them out of here. Take them away, those corpses!"

He pretended not to have heard me. He left the room. I looked around. There was Neruda's bleeding body. Heavily-armed soldiers danced in a circle around him. Gypsy bands lit fires under the body of Lorca. The eyes of my old friends – the coffee-house intelligentsia, I mean – are scattered around like bullets. They are planted motionlessly in every lifeless corner. I try to put my hand into the fire. It touches something hard and sticky. I draw it back to make sure I have not wounded or burnt myself and I see the eye of Nietzsche resting in my palm. It seemed to be crying from the pain and I could hear its sad lament. I felt a surge of hatred for those who were still able to cry. They had that curious comfort of being able to pour out their tears.

I told my husband what I had seen. He replied:

"Sleep . . . Try to get some sleep."

Had he forgotten that sleep to me was just an eery silence? It was out of the question on the field of an undeclared battle.

Little by little, I tried to forget. I even found some peace of mind, thanks to the double doses of Valium which I was receiving. Once again I was pushed back into 'normal' life – that's what they call it – and I began to read – should I say 'devour' – the cadavers of authors and their verses. I received my comrades when they called round to see how I was. I helped my mother with the cooking. When I saw she was sad, I would make fun of her, saying:

"Are you still praying for me, Mama?"

She would smile and say:

"You are in need of my prayers. I wish that God would guide you and give you back your senses."

As far as my mother was concerned, I had gone completely and utterly mad. How could a girl who had everything – a good marriage, a beautiful house, money – how could she spend all her time chasing the cares and tribulations of this world? My family tried to convince me to stay away from dangerous situations, particularly since Ayntab had begun to live in anxiety with acts of violence happening all around the town. I asked Issam, during his first visit to me after his escape from Harran, whether I could go back to my old job in the camp as soon as I was able to go out again. I missed those open faces and I knew all about the misfortunes and difficulties that they had suffered. After three months away, I felt a great sense of relief at the thought of going back to normal life. Instead of reading – devouring, I should say – the bodies of my friends, the poets and writers, I would go to my office in the morning and immerse myself in the everyday details of the lives of people who had remained, in spite of everything that had happened, unarguably real. One could always cast doubts on Aristotle and Hericlitus, and Costas Acselus, but you cannot ignore the onset of winter, or the threat of rheumatism and fever to the people of the camps. A strange longing for sunshine inhabited my body and it settled in the place where the foetus used to be. I was surprised how easy we find it to fill our bellies with lies and food, with living and laughter . . .

My baby died!

I was in the depths of wretchedness and exhaustion. For a time I had believed my baby had dark eyes, like the sons of the East. I had dreamt of birth and life inside me – I, who for so long had been locked in an embrace with death. As usual, I tried to lose myself in the memory of Abu Mashour.

Dark moments passed over me when I put my hand where the foetus had been. I felt it alive. I felt it kicking its feet against the walls of darkness, screaming, stroking my face, trying to lift the burden of life from my shoulders.

Khalid tried to change our lives, to break down the walls of silence and ice between us. He said to me:

"You are still young. You can have another baby."

He did not let me know the whole truth, however. He did not tell me that the gynaecologists had pronounced their judgement on my case: she will never be a mother. All I shall be is the lover of a child's face who will never be here. Ever since that time, I considered the defeat in Harran a personal vendetta which I have been living. One day I shall be able to take my revenge.

The days passed slowly while I was confined to the house. Khalid's face reminded me of the life which was going on without stopping on the other side of the walls. The faces of my mother and father return me to the sea and the olive groves and holm oaks. Poetry books rebuild bridges between me and my past once again. In poetry alone could I find my tranquillity. Through the brave words of Neruda, I regained the face that I had lost in the tragedy.

I was dogged by a yearning to return to the refugee camps. I yearned for the women and children, for the sun which washed away my fear of death and which had come to inhabit my veins. How difficult life becomes when you are waiting for your object of yearning.

The comrades were rebuilding their strength in Ayntab and the Palestinian camps bore as many children as there were stars in the sky. We were waiting for these children to grow and for rifles to bloom in their hands. I had a long wait. I was waiting for the day when the doctors would allow me to return to my usual life. I could not wait any longer.

My comrades, with whom I shared war and fear, and the refugee camps, come to me in the cold evenings and talk about the hardships which rule their lives. The Arab battleground has changed. The bridge of dreams which used to bind us together has fallen. The rosary was broken and the beads were scattered on the ground. Compromise was everywhere. It even reached our own ranks, and many succumbed. When I asked Issam about my future, he said to me:

"Why, you'll go back to the information bureau. That is where you are needed."

There was another reality that I was living: again I thought of the death of my child. Just a month or two before. I don't remember when exactly. I remembered something that Abu Mashour had said to me, at the time when I was circling the skies looking for revolution and homeland, just over a year ago. We were on the gleaming tarmac of one of the airports of the world, and he told me that he could hear the cries of children in the air. He said it sounded like a mysterious, ethereal sound penetrating everything. I listened to see if I could hear them as well but I could hear nothing. That was the day that I told him that he was confusing his desires and reality. I was not moved by what Abu Mashour used to say to me in those days.

But it is *my* child this time. My child, whom I carried inside me for three months. He shared everything with me; my love, my trips to the camp, my work on those ideological publications. The baby's decision to resign from this life so prematurely gave me a little consolation. I took it as a sign of his grief about what had happened in Harran. He could not face that kind of shame. It was a sign of his good faith – better than mine in that respect. For a while I dreamt of that dark-eyed child of the East. I wanted him to be a male child because we do not have enough men any more. I was insistent on creating a man, on bringing one into the world. I would look at every face I saw with hope, I would study it, and I always came to the conclusion that, after the Fifth of June, all our men had fallen to the bottom of a pit of fire where Medusa had turned them into black stones which could no longer move or love.

I would look to Abu Mashour for consolation. I would seek his face in my memory and find refuge there. Why did it have to be like that? Why wasn't he by my side? It seems to mean that he was not the best of men. But he was; that is why he picked up his things and went to his death.

My husband, the official one, who was calm and intellectual, who loved Johann Strauss and Saint-Jean Perse, carried on living his life's strange rhythmical tranquillity, with events that turned everyone else's lives upside-down hardly affecting him at all. Up at seven. Breakfast. The morning paper. Off to work. The sound of the car at exactly five minutes to eight. I could have set my watch by his car ignition. The motor again at three o'clock in the afternoon. Lunch and then into the bedroom and a few verses of Ezra Pound, whom he admired greatly.

"Draggled by griefs, which I by these incur,
My every strength turns my abandoner,
And I know not what place I am toward,
Save that Death hath me in his castle-yard."

My confinement at home allowed me a glimpse into my husband's life and his habits. There was no doubt in my mind that he had chosen his comfort and safety. He was his own homeland. The wider homeland around us meant nothing to him. I told him this one evening over supper. He remained completely unmoved, calmly finishing off his piece of French cheese. He had to have a piece of French cheese at the end of his evening meal, my husband. We could try to bring our bodies closer to each other in bed, but I found it impossible to become one with this kingdom of resolution and decisiveness, this world of numbers and split second timing. My God! How long had I been living with all that?

One of the savage summer nights of the encampment up in the north. Nothing was left of the night but an hour or two. I was never able to tell the time. Abu Mashour came to me in my tent with the latest communiqué from the leadership in Harran. It contained orders to move on to another location in order to complete our training before our mission to Europe. I stretched lazily in my blanket on the ground. Suddenly I felt the sharp pain of a thistle pricking into my leg. I must have missed it when I was clearing the ground for my bedding. I sat up with a start. I watched the blood trickling slowly and pleasurably down my thigh. I said to Abu Mashour:

"Even our blood complies with the awful progression of life. Why does a man die when the blood flows out of his body?"

He smiled at me and said:

"Death can be with you, just like life."

Our blankets were filthy yet our situation was spotless in its purity and our bodies were joined together while the smell of the earth crept onto our skin. A small moment of magic on the side of a hill covered in olive trees. When we saw each other's faces in the first light of the sun, we smiled and quickly gathered our belongings. We were parted and we didn't know whether tomorrow would bring us together again.

My husband chose his own inner peace. His own inner homeland. He built a fence around himself and there lived in peace. But what sort of peace did that afford? One day I asked him:

"Why did you marry me, Khalid? You knew perfectly well that I . . ."

He interrupted me before I could finish what I was saying:

"I wanted to see poems in you that I had not read before. I wanted to show you how life can be lived at its own pace and how we do not have to try to leap over history."

Once upon a time Khalid had been part of the struggle, but by now he was nothing more than a jumble of emotions looking for an inner peace which he thought could protect him from the terrifying jungle where we live out our existence.

Issam came over to our house on New Year's Eve, 1971. We went out onto the balcony and looked down over Ayntab. The whole town stretched away below us, throwing the tresses of its hair into the sea as it drew its body out of the water. The scent of orange blossom is mixed with the stink of salt and fish, swamping our words. The smells seem broken up in the midst of these celebrations of a defeated people. Celebrations of the losing side are hard to bear. They seem like bad funerals which fail to convey a holy and reverent sorrow about death. Issam looked at me and said:

"We have decided to carry out some more external operations."

I could not believe my ears. I thought that they had put that behind them for good. The strategy had done its job and we ought to be moving on now. That's what I thought, anyway. In fact, when the adventurers and scandalmongers got involved, the whole thing became a mess. The first operations were necessary to pierce the wall of silence which was put around us by the Western and Arab media. But the events of September in Harran had convinced me that our fundamental base had to be the Arab masses. There was no sense in our going further afield. With the words of Abu Mashour on the eve of the Geneva operation ringing in my ears, I said:

"No, Issam. Don't go back to that kind of operation. They just don't work any more. What we must do now is concentrate on spreading the struggle among the Arab peoples. We must unite with the masses of our host countries. If the fighting breaks out again here, we will have no one to turn to but them."

It was as though Issam had not heard a word that I had said.

"I have come to ask you to take part in the planning and preparation of three missions which we intend to carry out during the next couple of months in Europe. You have got insights into this kind of operation which will be lacking in those who do not have the benefit of your experience."

I tried to keep myself as calm as I could, and not to scream in his face. But I was thinking: Will you ever be able to face up to the truth?

Why can't you learn from your mistakes instead of just repeating them over and over again? Doesn't what happened in Harran tell you anything? The mass of the Arab peoples have abandoned us!

Issam was aware of the brooding silence within me. He asked:

"How do you see these matters then, Nadia?"

"It's very simple. What you must do is concentrate your forces in the south, close to the Occupied Land. There you must build up a revolutionary climate which will get the people rallying to the cause. As things stand at the moment, when the bombs start dropping on people's homes, the first thing those people will do is kick us out. That is what happens when they have no real reason to drive themselves to self-sacrifice."

Issam began going through the same old sickening phrases which I had heard so many times before: the self-sacrifice, internationalism, pan-Arabism. I looked at his face and was horrified to see that he now looked exactly like my old leaders in the party I had once been a member of.

I went with Issam to the military command and I made it very clear what I thought of them. I told them that I no longer believed in taking our struggle out into areas that did not directly concern us. I told them that the operations which we undertook in the past only served to obscure what was going on within our own sphere of combat. That was where the only reality was as far as I was concerned. I also told them I hated to see people treating me like a superstar, while all the time our comrades were dying without so much as a whisper about their sacrifice. I told them about my memories of the women and children who got caught up in our deadly operations and how their voices still haunted me. I remember a woman at London Airport shouting, "Haven't you got children of your own to fear for?" That day my answer was that our enemies did not allow us to have children.

But things had changed, and my comrades had to face up to that. Ayntab was not Harran. 1971 was not 1969.

They were silent, staring at me like imbeciles. Then they started to lay down their plans for the coming months, starting with the hijacking of an airliner. I attempted to raise an objection but Naif interrupted me, saying:

"Comrade Nadia. We are grateful for what you have achieved for our struggle and there is no shame in being weary of it now. Don't worry, we are not asking you to do anything in the active operational side. We just want the benefit of your experience and it is your revolutionary duty to offer it to us."

I was horrified by what I was hearing. I felt a sickening stab to my innards. I picked up my papers and stormed out of the room. This is how I parted company with them. I walked alone in the humidity of the night of the seaside town. I had to be aware that, from that day on, I was to face the world on my own.

In the following days, the rumour spread that I had left the Organization on account of personal reasons and people said that I could not carry on the struggle because of my health. I was prevented from getting into contact with the military camps and I was similarly banished from the refugee camps. In a nutshell, I was finished.

The first days passed with extreme difficulty. I spent the nights staring at the ceiling of my room, with Khalid by my side asking me to forget about it and to devote myself to my writing and to living my own life. He did not know how hard it is to forget. I couldn't escape the sharp pain which the slightest memory of what had happened caused me. It is as though the comforting ability to dream is dismissed and I am always brought back to the pulse of existence and reality, which I recall as the sleeper recalls a painful dream. The night that I came home after parting with them, I collected all my cuttings and papers that I had kept about the hijackings, the testaments to my courage, all the other little things which had only a personal, sentimental value, carrying that smell of a world where I had lived in my own personal vortex before the passing of the days convinced me that no good would come of it. I gathered together everything that I could find and I burnt the lot in the fireplace. I sat and watched the flames with an air of perfect calm.

The days passed with me looking everywhere for the truth which held me up and all the time I was tense with anger and the fear of being alone. I paced up and down the house like a *jinn* looking for something that I had lost. I faced a spiritual storm which upset my sense of balance and equilibrium. I discovered that I lived by a set of values which bore no relation to those of my husband. I reverted to my desperate search in books and the revolutionary heritage, and I found that I was separated from them by a bottomless chasm. An unworldly flood had picked us up and deposited each of us on a mountain somewhere on this planet. I loved my comrades and my revolutionary forebears like I loved my weapon, I knew them as well as I knew myself, and I sincerely hoped to be mistaken in my view of the way things were. My only consolation was the satisfaction that I was in the right and that what I did was in the interests of the struggle and the future of our revolt.

Five months passed after the split. I lived with the real pain of separation and alienation which overwhelmed my soul. My comrades had worked their way into my life and my thoughts and into my deepest emotions. For five months I was so near and yet so far from them and they received strict instructions not to contact me. I heard, or rather I saw in the papers, that they carried out two of the three hijackings that were planned, and that both ended in tragic circumstances. Three of our comrades died in the first one and both resulted in a number of our fighters being expelled from a European country with little or nothing to show for their efforts.

Five months passed, with Khalid living his symphony of inner peace. I, on the other hand, was like a burning coal smouldering in the corner of the spacious house. The bread was the colour of ash. The sky was the colour of ash. Joy itself was the colour of ash.

I tried to get back to normal life. I went with my husband to see his friends. I read the corpses of writers and picked over their philosophies. But I found it hard to succumb to the order of everyday life, just as everyday life refused to find a place in it for me. The friends' faces seemed colourless. We went out to eat in the restaurants of Ayntab where I was given beautifully presented helpings of poison. The nights were long and cold, filled with the unknown, and the cries of children in the camps, and the victims of Harran. I would have gone to the ends of the earth to rid myself of the terrible suffering which I was living in Ayntab. One day Khalid came to me and told me that his name had been put forward for a delegation which was to be sent to France. I said without hesitation:

"I'll go with you!"

He was very pleased. He had hardly expected that I would want to come with him. We packed our bags and I said farewell to my mother and father. I left Ayntab with a resolution which I had come to make during the long period of loneliness: to forget . . . to forget . . . to forget.

That is how I came to Paris, to search for the woman who inhabits my blood. But it was all in vain. I never really left home. Every night I found myself back among them. The body of my husband was the vessel which took me back. . . .

It was as though Harran was mapped out for me on the streets of Paris. It sprang out at me at every street corner. Every time I crossed the road, every time I looked over my shoulder to see whether someone was following me, to arrest me and take me to prison . . . Paris became Harran. Every time I saw a traffic policeman, the German prison vaults exploded inside me and a shiver convulsed my whole body.

In the first days of my life in Paris, I remained indoors. Khalid would go off to the hospital in the morning and leave me in bed, trying to conquer the first hours of lethargy which overtook me at dawn. I spent every night staring at the ceiling. My husband would say to me:

"Sleep. Your health can't stand this for very much longer."

I would try to sleep. I would pretend to sleep. But my eyes would keep searching for those forgotten islands which I had deserted. The search would go on until morning.

In the home I tried to play the housewife. I tried to look after Khalid's and my little affairs. I tried to read, and to write. But I failed, and my life became like a platform at the station, waiting for a traveller who was coming to me, but how, when and why, I did not know. The lie of settling down seemed like a tragedy to me. My bags remain unpacked and closed. I go to them every time I need something. I open the case, take out what I need, and then close it again as quickly as possible, waiting for the hour to come when I decide to go back.

Despite the noise of Paris, I could hear my comrades' voices raised in anger, their arguments, their tone of voice, reminding me of my own voice. I try methodically to train myself to forget.

Two months after my arrival in Europe, I wrote a long letter to Mary-Rose, asking her how she was and what was happening in Ayntab. I got a brief note back saying that they were under siege and that the battle was looming in front of them. She finished off by telling me to look after my health and to try again to have a baby. I could not understand why Mary-Rose should be going on about babies and my health. It was possible that the leadership of the Organization had made everyone believe that I had chosen family life before my life as a fighter in their ranks. They would not have mentioned the differences we had had. Certainly, Mary-Rose's letter contained nothing that indicated she knew what had happened between us. So I wrote her a lengthy letter explaining the circumstances of my departure and my current convictions about the best way for the Organization to proceed. I did not receive a reply.

Ayntab was on the verge of being burned to the ground and I was sitting here trying to forget. I just want to lead an ordinary life. I go shopping and I buy lots of things and I bring them back home with me. When I lay them all out in front of me, I am struck by the triviality and stupidity of what I have done so I take all the various articles and smash them or tear them up, then I throw the pieces away.

I tried to bring the house back to life. I tried to be a wife and to forget that I had been forsaken in the field of combat of the Arab cause. I live my new life . . . my new reality. I forget. But the picture of Abu Mashour remains with me. I see him everywhere. Sometimes I would see Ali Carlo or Farhan. I could see their eyes in the shadows as I walked around the Gare d'Orsay where we were living. The roads and windows all seemed to be blocking my path. My comrades were inside my body and they turned me into a moveable battleground, which is more dangerous than a fixed one. Silence inhabits us, or rather, each of us is inhabited by our own silence. Khalid started to stay away from the flat for longer periods. His daily walks became longer. Was he too looking for something which he had lost? One day he came to me with his composure destroyed. He was tired and drunk. He fell into the bed and tried to penetrate the wall which I had built around me. Then, in a moment of lethal silence, he said to me:

"Don't you want to try to have another baby?"

It was a question and a desire that I had completely forgotten about.

"Can't we talk about it some other time?"

This made him so angry that he shouted in my face:

"It was you that killed the baby! You and your bizarre lifestyle. That's what killed it. And now, when at last you have the chance to settle down and live a normal, natural life, you refuse. Aren't you sick of all the suffering and this endless journey? Your only view of Europe is of the airports stained with blood and haunted by death. You found death in Harran. You abandoned everything to go with your comrades. And now look at you. What have you achieved?"

I could feel Khalid's words opening the gates of sorrow and the past. I got out of bed shaken. I threw my coat over my nightgown and went out on the street to find some relief for my body and my feelings of alienation. Their memory still drove me to the furthest extent. That night I roamed the streets of Paris as if I were crazed. I passed night-watchmen and the darkened windows of cafés. I put my back to the wall and screamed. The echo of my voice tore through the night and the walls, and it pierced the sleep of the dyspeptic gentlefolk. When I got home, I did not find my husband. There was a letter which said that he had decided to settle down in Europe, and that it was up to me to think about my own life and where it was going. Finally, he reminded me that, if I so wished, I could get a divorce from him through our embassy in Paris.

I laughed out loud at his letter. What I found particularly funny was the laws which still govern our defeated people, with our embassies and ambassadors, the tiny details and the clichés which everyone attends to and respects. What embassy? What divorce? I don't belong to any country. None of my three passports – or is it four, I can't remember any more – have the name of my birth-place in them. It wasn't even my name, the name of the woman he had married. The current one was given to me by one of the progressive Arab countries just before I travelled to Europe, to give me a better chance of avoiding the police dossiers and intelligence registers, all of which would have contained my real name. The day they issued the passport, their consul in Ayntab told me to try not to move around too much between countries. He also requested that I did not get involved in any political activity while I was here. I agreed because I was desperate to get as far away from Ayntab as possible to be set free, after my comrades had destroyed all the bridges which connected me with them.

I sat in the flat alone. I thought about what I had to do now that Khalid had made up his mind to flee to the realms of his own personal peace, far away from anything which might remind him of our homeland, the homeland we had left behind at boiling point.

Should I go back to Ayntab? Should I perhaps settle down some-where in a corner of Europe for a while and try to forget and to get used to a life of exile. My comrades, my brothers, my only real family, have cut off all contacts with me. For some time I had not received any communication from Mary-Rose. I knew that Naif had travelled through Paris and had done nothing to get in touch with me. I had written a long letter to Issam, asking him to reconsider their position towards me, but stressing that I was not going to relinquish my view on external operations. I waited for a reply for a long time. Nothing came.

I had to decide quickly what I was going to do with myself. Cert-ainly, the comrades were not interested. It seemed I was alone; no one to decide my future for me; no one to tell me which road to take; no one to pay the rent for my flat and buy food; visits to the doctor alone; the petty realities of solitude in Paris.

I ended up working in one of the Arab embassies in Paris, (there are so many of them!) I hid my past from them, as well as my present. I rented a small room in the Fourteenth Arondissement and began writing countless letters to my comrades which I never finished. Daily life. The Metro. University corridors. The ladies next door. My bed, which was full of ice and alienation. I made up my mind to forget. I used to practise methodically. In the morning I would wake up and resolve to live my day. I leave my flat and drink a cup of coffee at a pavement café. I go to the office and dole out entry visas to tourists who want to go and gloat over our miseries. Occasionally I will tell them about *qat* and date-palms and, if I see them becoming more interested, I will try to sting them with a few of the shocking facts:

"You may not find proper toilet facilities to purge your overstuffed bellies out there . . . No, you can't bring your doggie into the country . . . Of course, you might easily get malaria or smallpox. . . . "

At the end of the day I pack up my sentences and contradictions and I go back home. There I pick over the corpses of books, and when the silence of solitude becomes too much to bear I may phone al-Bahi, and he will come over and perform his usual burial ceremony. We hold hands and walk along the boulevards, reviling everybody we can think of: rulers, leaders, writers, the political parties. Then we call our old friend Muhammad, the Ambassador of Hate, and we ask him out to a cheap supper in the Barbès Quarter, which is quite out of keeping with the country he represents, floating on oil, its fortunes being spent on indigestion and women.

I try to forget.

There are times when I come face-to-face with myself. My face is a face I have forgotten. I try to get close to it. I try to know the meaning of the days which I have lived and which I have yet to live. The wound inside me bursts again as soon as it heals, and oozes sorrow. I go back to poetry. On the pages I see my own face. It is old and grey-haired. I see the homeland in al-Bahi's voice. It turns into a glass of *araq*, a plate of *tabouleh* and the songs of Fairuz.

The only man . . . the just man, Muhammad, pulled me by the hand and led me back on crazy journeys into the desert. He talked about Umar bin al-Khattab and al-Mutanabbi and Ibn Damina. After that, he told me how he was happy to live by priorities which did not affect one another. He had discovered that we are all in need of priorities like that. It doesn't make any difference, because I live in expectation of oblivion.

Frank!

Tomorrow I leave Paris. I am waiting to return like the lover who waits for her beloved, the snow falling on her hair and in her eyes. The snow is here yet my body burns with the fire that tears through the silence of Ayntab. Gunfire pierces the flames, killing joy and dreams and expectation. The foundations of a savage kingdom are laid.

Before you and I met, like two bodies pulsating with blood and warmth – how odd that corpses should have pulses! – I was just about to land on the shores of surrender, living a daily reality in which I began to discover that it is hard to live without pain but that it is worse to live without joy.

The narcotic journey of forgetting ends up in a glass of brandy, the pages of a book, reincarnation of the soul, promised joy, the romantic poetry of Heraclitus . . . Nietzsche jabbering in the background . . . A friend calling me to ask how I am, just to make sure that I will still be around to bear their contempt.

Before you, I was addicted to my exile. I was addicted to oblivion. I was addicted to al-Bahi's funerals.

A burial accompanied by slogans in Arabic, the poetry of Labid, al-Shanfara, Urwa bin al-Ward. Before you, I was reassured by my friend Muhammad, the Ambassador of Hate. I would talk to him about faith and al-Sahrudi and Rabi'a. In short, I was addicted to a life without love and I roamed around until the pavements had become weary of my feet.

Not long ago, Muhammad said to me, while he was stroking my hair:

"What do you want out of life?"

Tears welled up in my eyes as I replied:

"To be safe from the rain. To be safe from people on the street, from passing cars."

He put his head on my lap. He kissed me on the knee. Then he lifted his face to look at me and said:

"I love you, Madame!"

I tried in vain to explain to him that love is a device of possession whose whole vocabulary is based on a tissue of lies. He did not believe me and started declaiming verses from Urwa bin al-Ward, and Tarafa, and Muhiyy al-Din Ibn Arabi.

Frank . . . You came to me through the groves of ice . . . through the nights of fire and vagrancy in the airports of the continents. You made the misery of memory explode inside me. How hard it is for those who have history and memory to bear the pain.

That is how we meet each other . . . how we met.

Do I love you? I don't know. You are like a great wave rolling towards the shores of oblivion. You carry the foliage of the jungle with you.

I become one with you. (I wasn't even at one with myself!) Together we talk about Nietzsche, Gide, Marlow, Althusser and Michaux. I used to try to integrate with people other than them – the comrades whom I loved. But what kind of integration was that? My inheritance is made up of blood and olive-groves and palm trees. Have you ever seen a palm tree in the middle of the ocean?

I tried to get your help. But it was hopeless. Many were the times that I sought the protection of your arms to try to keep the comrades out of my world. But death is death. My homeland is my homeland. And a civil war is not just an ordinary war.

They have woken up. Maybe they are waiting.

I am going back to Ayntab, even though I know that it is in flames . . . I shall join with them and we shall search together. We shall search through perils and dangers. We shall search through fire and death. We shall search for new horizons.

All my love,
Nadia.

Nadia collected her things and headed towards the door of the café. She left the drinkers and the warmth and *Le Temps des Cerises*, and she opened her heart to the night and the cold autumnal wind. She went round a corner in Boulevard Jourdan, passing through the Porte d'Orléans Metro station. She stopped at the corner of the street and listened to the noise of the night, a monotone at that hour. One of the vagabonds of the quarter passed her, leaning unsteadily, with a bottle of wine in his hand, spilling what was left of it over his head. She was afraid and quickened her pace. She lifted her eyes and surveyed the high windows, their curtains hanging down and the lights switched off behind them. There was hardly a soul left on the streets at that time. There was no more light to illuminate the world. With something resembling sorrow, she thought of Ayntab, which was ablaze and had not known sleep for a year. All the while the towns and cities of Europe slept without even being tired. Without that exhaustion . . . She turned into Rue Beaunier opposite the café where she habitually took her morning coffee. She went past Lenin's house, number twenty-four. For a while she remained fixed to the spot outside the pink stones which must have felt the fingers of the great man. She put her forehead against the wall and did not move. She thought of how she had stood transfixed for minutes on that spot when Frank told her about Lenin's first arrival in Paris. Nocturnal grief assailed her, as though she had only just finished burying a man whom she had loved. But Lenin had been dead a long time. He had died without coming to Ayntab and she was compelled to come here instead. She spoke another language. It was other faces she cradled in her arms. She lived other days in order to get to know him well.

She tried to collect her voice inside her, to launch it into the human desolation which surrounded her. To repeat everything she heard with her ears to make certain that it had been said, and to be sure that she was still alive and that the blood was still coursing through her veins. But she found that her voice had escaped her, betrayed her. She remembered that her house was in the other street and she had to pick her body up and hurry to her bed to sleep, so that she could awaken tomorrow to run after the Metro of death and live through the tiring day.

Suddenly she remembered her insect. The moment she thought of it she became fixed in front of Lenin's house. She stretched out her hand and pressed it against the wall to stop herself from falling over. She will return home, and there she will confront the insect and listen to it and she will warm to the familiarity of its voice until the daylight comes. She might find that the wall has already collapsed. Maybe the insect will have reached the pictures of her parents, the map of her homeland. With any luck it will not have managed to get the whole of the homeland down its throat and she will find that it has choked to death.

Nadia felt a little ease when this thought occurred to her.

A man passes her on the other side of the road, through the last hours of the tiring night. He thinks that she is one of those women:

"Come with me baby. I'll pay whatever you want. My house isn't far from here."

He grabs her arm forcefully. She screams. She frees herself from his grasp and runs in the direction of Rue Henri-Regnault. She stops in front of the door of number six. She is alone and out of breath. She looks over her shoulder. The man has not followed her. The only trace he has left is the echo of his laughter piercing the shadows of the night.

She climbed the old wooden steps hurriedly. She stopped in front of her door for a moment. She searched in the darkness of the stair well for the light. The monotonous noise of the insect reaches her from inside the room. She panics. She turns to run away. But where can she go? The town was asleep. All the café doors were closed. Frank was far away . . . in another continent. Muhammad would be deep in the embrace of his beautiful wife, bathing in the warmth of petrol. Al-Bahi had been out of her life for months, having stopped performing his funerals for her. He'd had enough and one day had said to her:

"I'm looking for another role. I don't want to be a grave-digger all my life. There aren't many decent corpses around these days, anyway, and you were one of the best."

She appealed to her courage which had lived with her in the days of the secret, undeclared war that she fought against a thousand phantoms and masked figures. It was no good. She thought back to the sun of the East, and the threshing-floors of her town beside the sea. Piles of silvery straw, hundreds of snakes mating together in peace. It was no good. The insect was of another order entirely. Gathering up all her cowardice and anxiety, she kicked open the door and went inside. She undressed and got into bed. Tomorrow was going to be a big day. She began counting . . . one . . . two . . . three . . . no sleep . . . Her eyes stared at the radiator and her insides quivered with sorrow and despondency.

"I will sleep tonight. What do I care about this insect? What if it does eat through the wall? Let it chew up my parents' pictures, Frank's face, my homeland, if it wants. It can bring the whole wall down, for all I care. It wasn't me who built it. So what if they kick me out of the flat. I'll find another place which doesn't have an insect. I might even leave Paris. . . . "

She turned on the light and her eyes looked around the room once again. The coldness of a single woman's bedroom. Cold, empty, nothing there. Colder still are the rooms of women who only sleep with their husbands as a duty. The flowers are dead in the flower-pots. Her bed is like a sea whose waters have been drained away.

Just as sleep was about to come, she remembered that she had got into bed without taking off her shoes. She turned the light on again. She saw the cigarette ends and the pipe lying in the corner. She could smell him in the room. She looked in the mirror and saw a woman's face, a woman she had met by chance by the wall of a cemetery. The woman was weeping silently. When she asked her why, the woman replied that she was crying for the town which had died from neglect. She breathed with joy. Why didn't she try to weep for the whole world? That had also died from neglect. The woman's eyes became narrower with the tears and the sobs. They became narrower and narrower until they were no longer visible in her face. She touched the place they had been and she felt a shiver sweeping over her whole body. At that moment the noise of the insect faded. She turned the lights out again and tried to sleep.

Sleep was a peevish partner which did not come to her easily. It remained aloof like her distant homeland, requiring forbearance and begging for revolution. She put her hand on her forehead. It was as cold as ice. The noise of the insect. The noise of a storm outside. The noise of windows shutting. Abu Mashour's face appeared to her, the sad face of a traveller who had gone without saying goodbye. He came up to her. He seized her hand. Harsh looks lingered in his eyes. She heard his voice coming to her.

"Where is your salvation, Nadia? Here you are, the leftovers of a woman . . . of a homeland . . . of a fighter."

She looked for excuses:

"At night, I shiver with the cold. . . . "

He asked the same question again, turning it around.

"Where do you think it is that you are escaping to? You go from one land to the next, one port to the next, looking for the struggle in other people. The struggle is within you. It is your responsibility to bring it out."

Nadia hesitated. She did not want to listen.

"At night I sit and dream of revolution, but in the day I find myself being drawn into the rat race."

No reply came from Abu Mashour and in a moment he was gone. Those sad eyes had gone off again to other horizons. Nadia found herself breathing a deep sigh of relief.

She tried in vain to sleep. The noise was still there. Now the sound of the insect was intermingled with Abu Mashour's voice, and her mother's distant prayers. She felt as though the life was being drained from her body.

"That's quite enough delirium for one night," she said to herself and she closed her eyes.

Nadia woke up the following day to the noise of the telephone. She was still immersed in the dreams of the previous night, the horror, the sudden lucidity, her realization that things were finished with Frank. She had lost him at the same time that she had lost her awful serenity, the moment she had ceased surrendering to life. Her search for oblivion and her desire to run away had lost their edge.

She lifted the phone and Frank's voice came on the line from far away. It was torn by the distance. It was torn by the heat of the continent which he was on at that moment. He said to her:

"The sun is very hot here . . . your image is with me here . . . I'll come back very brown. . . . "

She did not answer. He went on speaking:

"I waited for you to come. Couldn't you get any time off . . . ?"

Again she said nothing.

"I met some old comrades . . . I saw faces that I haven't seen for a long time . . . It really took me back. . . . "

She wanted to shout at him that his memory was dead inside her, that the funeral was carried out the day before. But the longing enthusiasm in his voice stopped her.

"Talk to me, Nadia. Say anything. What have you been up to? How have you been feeling?"

Finally, she spoke:

"I miss you, Frank, but I don't want you back."

He knew that these words meant that it was the end. She could hear the disappointment in his voice and she wished she had not spoken those words.

"Frank. After you left, I went to see a psychiatrist. He told me that I was like a wounded homeland which wanders through this world . . . He said to me. . . . "

"Wait for me . . . I'm coming back tomorrow."

Nadia put down the receiver and hurried to get dressed. She was late for work. She ran to the Metro station. She went past the café at the end of the street where she used to meet Frank during the cold evenings. She recalled that he had abandoned her. When she reached Place de Bercy, she looked up at the statue of Joan of Arc and she gazed upon the pure and clear face of the saint. She went into her office and started to organize her papers. She had made up her mind, that day she would end all her relationships in Paris. She would go to her boss and tell him that she was leaving. She would go back to Ayntab, back to her comrades. There she would either create her own revolution or die in the attempt. She wrote her letter of resignation and felt calmer. For the first time since she went into exile, she felt that she had finally found a port-of-call, a harbour in which she could weigh anchor. She walked into her boss's office and without a word she handed in her resignation. He stared at her without seeming to understand what she was doing.

She walked straight out of the building. She crossed the Place du Trocadéro stopping for a while to look at the many statues which were around her. She had been like a statue herself. She had been dead and now she was coming back to life.

In a turning leading to Avenue Henri Martin, where most of the Arab embassies were, waiting with their characteristic air of casual, unconcerned idleness, she saw al-Bahi crossing the street. He signalled to her with his hand, and then he raised his voice and asked her whether she was still alive. She nodded and crossed the Quai de la Seine without stopping to talk to him. There she was in Place Dauphine, once again, trying to sniff its aroma, just as all prisoners do when they leave their prison cells. All Paris is prisons and cells . . . How can we talk about leaving then? She calmly took refuge by an old oak tree. She tenderly stroked its bark. She let the cold living wood caress her cheek. She tried to remove the dead leaves from around its base. Alone, like a stray cat, she runs, sticking closely to the trunks of trees, from one tree to the next. How was it that she had not in the past discovered how tender trees were. She hurries to the entrance of his building. She climbs the few stairs. She listens to the rippling of the Seine and the famous bitch of a film star yapping in her rooms. She thinks back to her face in one of the films, when she kisses her lover before stabbing him with a poisoned blade that she has been honing for days in the silence of her loneliness. The smell of decay pervades everything and it reminds her that she will be leaving.

The waters of oblivion were flowing from her body and washing against the walls and the floor which had witnessed the union of their two bodies. The torn canvas of the mariner, the picture of Frank in court, now cast on the ground like a dead body, all his things . . . his desk . . . his tobacco . . . his clothes cupboard . . . the manuscript of his latest novel. He was probably going to talk about her at the end of it. At least she'd provided him with some new material.

It is strange how things lose their significance . . . the things we love and the things which we think define our world.

She takes the papers on which she has been writing all through the previous night, puts them into an envelope and seals them up. Then she throws the package onto the desk on top of the manuscript of his novel. She is on the point of going out of the door when she stops for a while and stares at the clock. It says ten minutes to six. For as long as she had been going to the flat that clock had shown ten minutes to six. She picks it up and moves the hands to the correct time. But time was not watching her foolishness on this occasion.

In the past, time had frozen in her veins. Now the days had come to move on. It was time to strike the camp she had pitched in the shadow of his blue eyes, on the border between his body and her consciousness, she had killed off what was left of her life.

The flat was silent. The were no insects triggering in her head a desire to wage war or give up on life. No faces visited her in the night. In the flat there were all the signs that the owner had made peace with himself and with all the disappointments and frustrations of this world.

She goes down the stairs to the square once again. She sees the face of the owner of the Algerian restaurant at the entrance to the building. She acknowledges him with a nod of the head and then she hurries off to the Palais de Justice. She goes up the steps to the imposing entrance of the building. She touches the wall. The building was still in its place, but anyone who wanted to find some justice there would have to search for a long, long time.

Where to now?

For the first time she asks herself that question. In the past she would go to work without thinking, or to Frank's flat, or to her own flat. But now she is left wondering where to go. She discovers that she has a capacity for questioning which she had forgotten in the past.

She stops for a minute or two in front of one of the riverside shelters and stares at the waters which are swollen by the recent rains.

To her right she can see Notre Dame cathedral, impermeable to surprise, an eternal witness to the continuity of life.

Why does Paris seem bigger now than she was accustomed to seeing it. Why does Saint Michel look at her with the face of a child. There is a strange and unfamiliar feeling to this morning.

"I haven't arrived."

She hears her raised voice in the brutal, polished depths. She smells the aroma of the city and the river and she studies the faces of the people walking past her. She thinks about calling one of her friends in the city and telling them that she is going to Ayntab. But what was the point? Al-Bahi would miss her because he had no one to bury any more. Muhammad would say she made an excellent lunatic. Ahmad would raise his glass to the journey. In a day or two they would be steeped in the bodies of their wives and girlfriends again and her bed would still be empty. She hurries off to the nearest travel agent and asks to be booked on the first flight to Ayntab. A European man, who knows his job very well, stares at her like an idiot.

"Madame, didn't you know that there aren't any flights to that destination?"

"No flights to that destination." She repeats his words with a strange look of astonishment in her eyes. How could she have forgotten that there had been no flights to Ayntab since the war began? Where had she been? Could it be that she had forgotten the massacres which wash the streets and the blood which covers everything? Where had she been? She turned away from the face of the travel agent, who wasn't bothered by these issues and went out onto the street. She walked around aimlessly. When she found herself opposite the Café Cluny, she crossed the street and went to sit at a corner table.

She tried to pull herself together. It was essential that she find a way of travelling to Ayntab. Why not go to another Arab country on the borders of Ayntab and transfer from there to her destination? And if the authorities there didn't want her passing through their country . . . ? If they arrested her for her past political affiliations? Well she'd deal with that when it happened. She picked up her papers from the table and went out quickly in the direction of the travel agency that she had been at an hour before. She sat in front of the 'neutral' travel agent and asked him to book her on a flight to the capital of the neighbouring country. It did not take long and soon he was giving her a ticket for a flight that evening. She took it out of the man's hand and went quickly back to her building. At the entrance she came face-to-face with the neighbour who lived on the first floor. She nodded her head to him in greeting and went on up the stairs. She was determined to kill the insect and rid herself of it once and for all. Why not throw it out of the window? Whatever happened, she was definitely going to kill it. . . .

Returning to her comrades. She would start all over again with them. She had never felt at ease from the moment she left them. She had never stopped having to fight for her life.

When she opened the door, she found that silence prevailed in her room. No noise. No insect. No questions on the walls. She went up to the wall-homeland and took a look behind the radiator. She could not see her insect. It had packed its bags and had left without leaving a forwarding address. Perhaps it had already left for Ayntab and would be waiting for her there.

She looked for her genuine passport and when she found it she thumbed through the pages and then threw it into her bag. She looked around at the room. There was still a picture of Frank on the wall next to her bed and the smell of his body on her clothes and on her skin. But this time she was leaving the land which had brought them together, the land which had borne the weight of their bodies and had seen their joy. She was going to leave Paris and when she arrived at her destination she would remember it with a tinge of sadness.

"There's nothing for you here. Here there are dark corners while Ayntab is a burning coal upon the Mediterranean coastline. Going there is like going back to your mother's womb. Going there is like returning to the first revolution of your dreams."

She closed the door and went back down the stairs. Her footsteps on the old wooden steps brought her back to the sadness of the nights of solitude when she had searched for someone like herself, for Frank. For her marriage. For her real name. She said farewell to Rue Henri-Regnault, looking back at the old building where she lived. She remembered that she had forgotten to tell Anita and Miraille that she was leaving. But why should she tell them? Anita would ask tomorrow and Miraille would miss someone shutting the door at four o'clock in the morning. They would gossip about her for a few minutes, and then everything would turn to dust.

To the airport, by herself.

"No-one to see you off. Not to worry – your comrades are all waiting for you there."

His plane landed at Orly Airport. The plane which had travelled for many miles. The plane which had come from a hot country laughing in the face of the cold air of Paris.

Here you are, coming back to Europe, Frank. In your head you carry those images which have never really left you, although they have become distant and it is no longer possible to re-organize them in your imagination. They said to you as they were waving goodbye at the airport: "This country is your country. We will never forget what you have done for us and the days that you spent in prison on our behalf."

They had of course forgotten how different you were and how much you had changed. Now you are back in good old Paris. No more politics. You can shelter behind that Frenchness of yours, that great Frenchness which once drove you to the other side of the globe so keen were you to escape it. They waved you off and you waved back. But her voice had been with you all the time. It haunted you during the final days of your stay, her voice and her tired face which had seen so many unknown cares. Her eyes were traced on the water, changing their colour as they went back to the womb of bygone days. She approaches in a small ship carrying men who had come to change the face of history.

In the last days her eyes followed you everywhere. You saw her at the door of the guest house which they prepared for you. You saw her crossing the streets leading to the palace of the former dictator. You saw her in the square that had witnessed the revolution you helped to create. It vexed you that she was not by your side. When you called her to say you loved her, you heard the ice in her voice and your blood shivered as you tried to get a little warmth from the tropical sun.

"I miss you Frank but I do not want you back."

When a woman misses a man, it is because she has got used to having him around. When she yearns for him, it is because she is in love. She called out to him, that woman coming out of the East. The migratory bird did not come to roost in Paris by accident, nor was it attracted by the ancient stones of the Tuileries Palace. You spent much time wondering, without mentioning it, what a woman like her was doing here. She had talked a lot. She would talk to you about her mother and father, about the sea, about her husband, but she always kept a secret inside her which she was never able to divulge. She will be there at the barrier in the arrivals lounge, no doubt, waiting for you. No doubt she will be happy to have you back. No doubt she will bury herself in your embrace and say to you:

"I have missed you. . . . "

That would be enough. After that, the passing of the days will be sufficient to guarantee that things change.

He crossed the tarmac. There was a biting wind and he started to button up his coat. He put his bag down and fastened his woollen cardigan. Then he picked up his bag again and walked into the terminal building. He approached the airport security men and held out his passport. The official looked at the passport and let him through. He studied the faces of those waiting outside. He searched for her head among all the other heads, for the long night of her hair. For the fleeting daylight in her eyes. But there was no trace of her. She must have been held up a bit, or maybe she had got his arrival time wrong. He had sent a telegram two days beforehand and it should have arrived by now. He went forward a little, still looking for her face among the crowds of passengers and the people meeting them. But

Nadia was not there. She had not arrived. She had not arrived yet. He felt a lump in his throat and a thought flashed through his mind: Had she decided not to meet him? But why would she do that? Sure, she had been a bit strange on the phone, but that did not mean she had decided to split up with him. He went to the café on the second floor where they usually went when they were at the airport. He looked at all the customers. He stared at the faces of men and women. Nadia was not there.

He ran down the stairs and waited in front of the flight information board. He waited for half an hour. An hour. Finally he gave up hope and went out and hailed a waiting taxi. He threw himself down on the seat and told the driver to take him to her address.

"Before you left, Nadia was living a tragedy which she did not talk about and no one knew anything of it. Each time that her head teemed with questions, she would fold her arms over her breast and wait for you in the Place Dauphine, by a shelter between the Palais de Justice and the Pont Saint Michel. She had something to say to you, but she would always let her thoughts be dispersed in the darkness and she would remain silent."

The car was approaching the outskirts of Paris. He told the driver to take the route past Passage du Genty and Boulevard Jourdan. The driver carried on going as though he had not heard the directions which Frank gave. Then he started grumbling over his shoulder:

"You know life in Europe's pretty miserable, Monsieur. Look at the traffic . . . at this time of day! It drives you up the wall sometimes."

You think about the fact that you have just come from a land where people are driven by hunger. "And you are fighting for people's rights to have a second steak for dinner and two deserts," as Nadia had said when he told her why he was back in France. "We are fighting to stay alive. Your problems in Europe are different to those of the country that you have come from. Find a solution for the problem of the eight million cars in Paris, if you like."

The car stopped in front of Nadia's building and Frank got out. He paid the fare and ran quickly up to the second floor. He stopped for a moment at her door to get his breath back. He knocked but there was no answer. It was Saturday and Nadia was not at work. He knew her well enough to be sure that she ought to be at home. Was she ill? He knocked again a little harder this time and waited. Nadia's neighbour came out of the room opposite and when she saw who it was she smiled and said to him:

"I shouldn't bother, Monsieur Frank. Nadia left yesterday. She asked us to leave the key with the landlord. I've still got it if you want it. She's probably left some books for you. Do you want to have a look?"

He put his head against the wall. Then he turned on his heels and went down the stairs without speaking to the neighbour. He found himself in the daylight again, which was bathing the street. He ran over to the taxi rank and got a cab home.

He climbed the stairs to his flat, stopping on the third-floor landing which overlooked the Seine. That was where she would stop to look at the river and smile. She would look up at him, brush the strands of hair away from her face, and say:

"I can't understand you. I admit that I'm helpless."

He opened the door and a damp smell greeted him. The smell of a house where no foot had trodden since his departure. His eyes looked around the sitting-room and studied its contents. His clothes on the sofa, her nightdress hanging in the passage, the blue bathrobe which she used to wrap around her body . . . her smell mixed in with the other smells of the flat . . . his study where she used to spend hours scribbling words which he couldn't read. He threw his bag down and went to his desk where the cleaner had put all the correspondence which had arrived for him during his absence. He was leafing through the letters when his eyes fell on a large envelope on which was written in her handwriting:

"To Frank."

He ripped open the envelope and his eyes fell on the opening phrase:
"I know that it is wartime . . . "

He pulled up his chair and began reading. He became lost in the words. Cold sweat dripped down his forehead. After a while night fell and darkness covered everything. Frank turned on the light and carried on reading. Past days were illuminated in his head and he found himself once again in the worlds of total contradiction which he inhabited during his days in prison. What had she wanted from him? Why had she made this stop-over in his life? To what extent had she been struggling during her days here and how was it that he had not been able to understand?

He had always had grave doubts about her being just an ordinary woman. A student. That is what she had told him, but he had never really believed her. He had thought of her as one of those young women who could not manage in the Third World because the borders of their awareness went beyond their reality. That made them come to Europe in search of knowledge, experience and culture.

But she was gone now and he was still shackled to the limitations of his humanity. The conditions under which he had lived since his return from Africa were still in place. The bonds with his reality in France were not broken. His reputation was still here, his homeland, and, above all else, his daughter, Laurice, the love of his life from whom he would never be parted.

The wound on her shoulder. A bullet wound.

That day she smiled when she told him that it was a scar from an operation that she had had when she was a girl. He did not believe what she said but he had never imagined that she could be the woman on the front pages of a newspaper that he had seen when he was in gaol, the woman who had been involved in three hijacks before being captured in Germany.

How had she been able to hide that from him?

Was it all an attempt to forget, as she had said? Had she really forgotten?

"Ayntab is burning, Frank. It will go on burning for ever unless I return. I shall find my comrades there somehow. Our differences are behind us now that the battle has commenced. I must be reunited with them, for better or worse. I must join them in battle. We know that there will be nothing else for us in this world. We have made up our minds."

He went back to reading the words, his breathing coming with difficulty. He felt as though his feet were chained to the ground and his arms were tied to the sky. He felt his head was ready to explode.

"I was afraid that you would turn me into just another piece of material for your novels. I was afraid that you might write about me. 'She lived here, far from where the battle was raging.' You refuse to come to us. Your country needs you. This is what you said to me one day. Well, you can stay if you want. My country needs me as well and its too terrifying for me to cut my ties with it.

"These questions which dogged you, Frank, in a country where a revolution was as essential as water to drink and air to breathe . . . in a country whose goals became open guest houses and where blood washes the streets. I tell you I do not believe any more that there will be total revolution which will eliminate all iniquities. Every example which you have given us so far has ended up as a model of tyranny and dictatorship. I'm not trying to bring happiness to human beings but I am going to defend their lives. I am not fighting in order to change how they live. I am fighting to get them back their land."

He put the papers down on the desk and stood up. He began to pace around the room, looking for a release.

"You were far from our world, Frank. We needed your approval to make it easier for those who entered the Occupied Land and who never came back. But your approval was denied us, Frank, just as your doors were closed to us. I can't be with you, because I am washing my face, eating, sleeping, waking, working and taking care of my body in expectation of my return to him."

"I was just a stopping-off point, no doubt."

He said this to himself as he was going into the bedroom, where Nadia had torn up the canvas of the mariner and the picture of him in court. She had destroyed his present. She had executed him in the present and was determined to live with his past. She searched his face for the traces of revolution which she assumed would be there, but she had not found anything. Who had told her that there was a revolution? Who had told her that he had gone searching for that and not for himself?

He lay down on the bed and stared for a long time at the shafts of light which pierced through the door separating the study and the bedroom. He tried to speak. He wanted to shout out that he was not a prophet, that he was as cowardly and as weak as the next man, and that he had been afraid.

The moments burned and the mist of reality enveloped everything. He had set light to his dreams once in the heart of silence. The woman coming out of the fire . . . The woman coming out of the East, where she burned her boats and whence she came looking for her own silence.

But silence refused to be her ally, although it stopped her cries penetrating the walls.

He carried on staring at the ceiling of the room, remembering her face, remembering her eyes which were fiery with hope, her face which used to carry in its features her profound sense of alienation. Oh Nadia, we are both in exile, but where did you get the idea that I am still looking for revolution?

He is in his prison cell once again. The hot country. The prison where he spent those long days. The priest comes in to him moments before his execution. they have shaved his head and given him a loose white robe to wear. His ten crimes are written down the front of the garment.

1. Stealing the sky to blind their eyes
2. Stealing the rain to wash away the tombs.
3. Stealing the snow to make a river.
4. Stealing the distances to make an ocean.
5. Stealing the wombs of women to procreate.
6. Stealing the blood to tint the rain.
7. Talking of guns and of men who wished for death and life.
8. His passion for this world.
9. His love for Laurice.
10.

The place for the tenth crime remained empty. They had not worked out what it was yet. He told the priest that, while the latter was robing himself in artificial compassion. He almost told him what it was: his crime of loving a woman who bore a star on her forehead and carried her homeland in her eyes. She came out of the East, searching in our cemeteries for the answer to her problems and the problems of her homeland. The West slammed its doors in her face and her homeland had also locked her out. His crime was to be yearning for her at that moment, for her head which had taken him back to his past.

He was unnerved by the face of the priest before him. He wanted to give him a hearty slap on the back and tell him that he did not need to make his confession because his crimes were already written there on his chest, but the crime which had been left out was the most serious of them all, and the one which had condemned him to death.

The priest said:

"May your sins be pardoned, and may you take refuge in your Saviour. There is none but Him. After a short time you will be received by Him and you must therefore accept your death with courage. Confess to what you have committed. I am a father to you. I am the go-between 'twixt you and your Saviour."

Frank shouted fiercely in his face:

"I don't need you! Leave me alone! I don't have a saviour or a father. It is for me to accept death or to fight against it."

The priest went slowly out of the room and walked down the long dark corridor. Walking. No other sound. Not even from the chains which bind Frank's hands. The chains are silent as though they have been turned into transparent tears. The dungeon walls closed in on him once again, almost covering him. He remembered the vast sky surrounding the leafy city. He remembered the banana trees outside which throw their arms to the neighbouring forests. The sounds of the animals screeching and barking with joy. He tried to break the chains but they were too strong. There was nothing he could do to free himself. He heard a light knock on the door of his cell. It opened and the cell was filled with the smell of wild leaves and grasses.

Nadia entered. Her head was crowned in a halo of fire. Her eyes were like two seas of the night. Her black hair was like the night which seeped into the cell from a hole in the top corner of the wall. Nights in prison do not have stars. She was dressed in white like a bride of the sea. Beautiful and alluring, she waited for him to approach her and to place a kiss on her forehead, the greeting of those who meet in places of exile far from home.

The tenth crime had come to him there in the dungeon. Joy and sadness. What had brought her there? Why was she in white? A garment to wed her to his blood. A garment of birth and procreation. There she is, the trace of sadness, which she always wore, now but a memory. What a turbulent woman you are! He tries to approach her but the chains on his legs hold him back and keep him shackled to the wall. He wants to spread his arms and embrace her. He wants to shout for joy. The storm outside is laying waste to the cities. The shame of our humanity. The fear of our rotting insides.

"Nadia, I didn't confess this time. I did not tell the priest about my tenth crime, about you. I waited for you in the nights between the dungeon walls, and when my hands were not chained I drew your face on the wall, on my clothes, on the ground, on the rain, on the night coming in through the hole. The guards found your face everywhere and they took it away to ensure they killed love more effectively. They stole it just as they had stolen truth and they turned it into dust. They stole it like they stole the birds of winter in order to wake the trees. They stole it to entertain the night, in order to live their deaths more effectively.

"Oh, Nadia, you made death wait but your fate was predetermined."

He tried to tell her that he was hungry and that he felt the need to be nursed at his mother's breast, that he was yearning for the trees of death. But his voice let him down. He was angry, tormented, agonized. Terror . . . Revolution . . . But there was no way that he could express these violent emotions which were surging through his body. And Nadia was still standing there at the entrance of the cell with the storm raging behind her. Her face was unblemished, without a trace of pain, touched by the Eastern sun.

"Let her who comes to me speak."

Her lips did not move. Her head remained still. An enigmatic smile was all that could be seen on her lips. The smile washed over the icy cell. Set free, it erased the traces of torture from his body. She made him want to howl with the wolves in the distant forest.

He gathered his strength and shouted at the top of his voice. He heard his cries echoing around the room and he opened his eyes. He was lying in bed. He looked up at the ceiling and at the room around him. Everything was in its place. His flat in Paris. His books were lying in the corner, sobbing in the silence. The dumb insolence of his typewriter. His daughter's photograph. The torn canvas on the floor. He moved his arms and legs, lifting them off the bed one by one. No chains. No shackles. He explored his body. His hand stopped at his chest and stomach. There was no white robe and no list of crimes.

He watched the rays of sun streaming across the beams of the room. He heard his deep voice, a voice from those far-off days, ring out:

Do you really want to leave again. Four years waiting for the moment of your execution. Every time the door opened you thought that they were coming to take you away. One day a priest came in to ask you to confess your sins. You wanted to tell him that it was all a mistake but instead you hit out at him and turned your face to the wall. For a long time you did not eat, you did not speak to anyone, you didn't even turn around. You kept your eyes fixed to the wall in expectation of the moment of death.

Three years before prison, while you were carrying papers from one city to another, in different places on the continent, the sun burning your skin, Paris would come to you across your dreams. Your room in the big house waiting for your return. Your friends asking you where you are.

And Miraille. She was a comrade you were in love with. She used to meet you outside the city. Her brown face. The long tresses of her hair. She brought you the latest publications thrown up by the hopeless intellectuals in your country in their attempts to eliminate their ineffectiveness and impotence.

You ended up by yourself. When you faced your enemies, you found that you had no friends in the world other than yourself. You bore a lot. There were some attempts from abroad to get you released. A succession of faces coming to you until you were finally free. They took you in the dark night through the streets which were full of poverty and hunger and they threw you, like a contraband suitcase, onto the first plane going to your mother country. When you set foot on French soil, you swore that you would never leave her again.

You arrived home. You climbed onto the vehicle of time and ease. You married Miraille with her long tresses and she bore you a baby daughter. You looked into her blue eyes and saw the sky. You were living in the lap of luxury now. But every time you heard a door slam or a window closing you jumped out of your skin. You went down like a shot bird when the sun struck your head, even though you knew that it was not as strong here as the sun in that country. Your comrades have died, you idiot, or they have been scattered to the four winds. You were a stranger in that distant continent. They made you a legend, and the victims of that legend were people like Nadia and her comrades. How do you escape from your past? Where do you go? You swore that you would never put yourself in dangerous situations again. You promised yourself a life of ease. A life breathing the air of freedom in Europe, reading the poetry of Louis Aragon, writing books and short stories.

But . . . she came to you like a cloud, like a tempest, sharp and clear. She tore up your silence and cleared away your oblivion. She reminded you of a burning place on this earth, while you had been luxuriating in the peace of Europe.

You were afraid of telling her that it was all over and that now it was the face of Laurice that you were bound to . . . the Place de la Concorde . . . your house . . . the Quais on the banks of the Seine. You were afraid to tell her that you were not what she imagined you to be. Her voice would wash away the layers that you had put around yourself for protection. You loved her as a woman and as a woman she rejected you, as a woman rejects a man. She left you in the lethargy of your ease and she escaped. She went off like a tigress, searching for the spot of blood on the forehead of her land. But she had sent you back to your past.

Revolution is not restricted to one single land.

Remember, this is what she told you as you were trying to convince her of your current point of view.

"Every freedom fighter on this earth is responsible for the lives of his comrades, no matter where they are."

Frank got up and went to the bathroom, seeking refuge in the hot water. If only he could get himself out of this train of thought. If only he could distance himself from this mania which was pushing him to the land where the battle rages. If only he could erase from his eyes the image of Nadia, lying face down, the gun-shot wounds decorating her back like medals. But the hot water only increased the sounds and thoughts burning in his blood and his head. Things now looked even more complicated than they did before. He had to make a resolution to rid himself of the duplicities which governed his life.

What about Laurice?

His mind was occupied as he dried off the drops of water on his chest. Will she live like an orphan? Who said she will live like an orphan?

He stared at the torn canvas of the mariner. He saw new sails coming over the horizons, sweeping angrily over the oceans before his eyes. He quickly dressed and went down the wooden steps to the town which he loved.

He crossed the street in the direction of the Quai de la Seine. Paris seemed cold and miserable that morning, with the gusts of wind blowing his hair this way and that. He got in his car and drove to the headquarters of his party. What was he going to tell them this time.

"It's all over. I have decided to leave France again."

They will probably stare at him in surprise. There are the elections soon and it is possible that the socialists might win this time. What will they say? That he has run away from the reality of his own land and has fled to another country. That he is now used to not having a homeland of his own, or a name, or an identity.

He had got used to being the consultant, the outsider. They will say. . . .

Well, let them say what they want. France does not need people like him. France will realize its profits whoever is in charge, Left or Right. History has given her the opportunity and her revolution was realized long ago. Here she is now, living in expectation of the achievement of even greater affluence. Institutions in France will be more democratic and revolutionary change will come as a result of the long history of a country which had already brought about change through its bourgeois revolution . . . As for Nadia, she has gone to a place where death waits outside the doors of time. Every day it knocks somewhere with its bloodstained hand, ready to snatch away a human being.

When he arrived at the Café Saint Clô, his hands slackened on the steering wheel. He could not carry on any longer. He parked the car on the Saint Germain side. He looked at Paris in the morning. It had not changed at all. It had not changed since the day he left it to go to that other country. The first hours of the morning. Like every morning the newspaper vendor was on the corner where Frank normally bought his newspaper. The church was still there. The picture seller . . .

The essence of Paris. That is how I imagined you in exile. She used to speak to me all the time that I was afraid.

He got out of the car and headed towards the Café Saint Clô. He crossed the threshold and was hit by the heat and the empty expressions. Boredom and turbulence. But the turbulence dies down. The eagle which spreads its wings to receive her was asleep on that Saturday morning in 1977. He knew the face of the waiter. He was there every morning. And the fat man sitting at the till. The old woman who had frequented this place for the last ten years.

And you used to come here, alone, your eyes ablaze, not able to face the frost of the political parties. The whole world sleeps under your memory. You try to force death to tailor itself to your measurements. Your vitality, your wonderings inhabit you from one dawn to the next. Eight o'clock at the library on Rue d'Ulm, you took your breakfast in the café opposite before you were woken up again by your questions. Sections of hell before going. Sections of hell after leaving. Sections of hell at your return. Sections of hell in the body of Nadia, which was engraved by torture. Rape in prison vaults. And a single woman loved you. A single woman parted company with you. She is the revolution which you searched for in your country and did not find. Calm down, Madame, I will not abandon you. You used to be afraid sometimes. Your mother used to look in your eyes. But you were in need. You needed to translate your body and your questions into action and you were sure about that need. The ceiling is in front of your eyes and your back stretches on the wooden floor of your room in the big house. Your blue shirt sticks to your body as you suffer the torture of your intellectual solitude and your alienation. Your hand is always tugging at a lock of your hair and the sounds of alienation issue from your throat. The game has ended – or has it just begun? You must go back again, whatever. Mr 'So-and-So' is against the revolution because the objective conditions are not yet secured. Stop. There is a change of routes, please. Much ease. My dear Western Marxist. In these sorts of cases, you have to make your decisions on your own. There is no-one to help you. You don't mean your leaders, with their puffed up stomachs and their constant mistakes. You make mistakes too, you know. The file is closed. Stop. Full-stop. You believed that there would never be revolution in your country. You were convinced and it was still impossible. Stop. For and against. The awareness of a fair, frail-bodied child. 1968. You wait. 'You naughty revolutionary'. Divorced from the revolution but in fact almost made for it. The high rooms and the bowed ceilings. René's face, coloured by Africa as he explains to you the consequences of your continued presence. You go to your party. Back to your leaders. Nine flights of stairs to the newspaper offices. Under the nose of the manufacturer of spite and justice and history. The road seems to go on for ever. No objective reality. You had to break your wings to forge them anew. After that the jungles, the comrade stabbed in the hot night between his prayers and his gun. His eyes looked towards your prison, and you saw him in yourself. You give him a name. You search for his face in the darkness of your solitude. You ask about his life. The land of his cross. His friends. You follow the paths of his body, his head and his soul. The paths of the spirit.

"Miraille. Was he really killed?"

Miraille held back her tears as she came to you with the face of the past. It was her first visit after your sentence was announced.

"He was crucified. A hundred spikes pierced his body."

You were embarrassed by the pain you felt, and you tried not to let your guards and executioners see it in those moments of loneliness. You became convinced of the impossibility of a revolutionary operating in a country other than his own, while part of your soul conspired to convince you of the impossibility of revolution itself. You pulled the white sheets from your bed and you tried to make a rope out of them. Questions. Question marks.

You heard fragments of lost poems by Aragon, obscure fragments of unknown origins. They came to you with the sunset which crept in through the hole in the highest corner of the wall. You were torn between your yearning for life and your hankering for death, the desire for liberty for many different men of this world. That is how you became so easily lost in the forests of your past. You drew a few spots of sympathy on the papers as a fair youth who had come from a distant land. Lighted spots like candles in a temple. At night you would wake up and see your steps across your cell – three metres long and two metres wide. You tried to write early in the morning. You tried to define the moment of the last breath. You couldn't, so you distributed it over the past and the present. You used to write, in an attempt to pierce the walls of your prison, in the belief that the dawn would come. That unknown day which drove you to wonder sometimes whether it really existed at all on the horizons of time.

The hand of night reached everything. Your guards. Your executioners. The sad *calaria roasa* growing on the other side of the wall. You are a living corpse in your cell. Deep, dark, black. You think of Paris and become immersed in the light of the Place de Dauphine.

The bright mornings when you had to draw the curtains before you could dream. The eyes of a man of thirty were cold wrinkles concealing nothing and revealing all. You became weak and you wondered if you would really be able to face the world again. You go over events without recognizing your failures. You try to be self-aware and self-critical. Sometimes you forgive yourself for having talked. The body which knew the snows of Europe could not bear the heat of their torture. You told them everything you knew. Your comrade was killed in the jungle after your confession. From that moment you were incapable of self-love. You tried to run alone in your cell. You tried to run towards repentance and purification. When terror ceased you found yourself face to face with your dead friend. You fell to your knees and called out his name.

"Oh, ever-loving Christ, I have finished bowing to you and I do not know what truth brought me here."

You were a child playing with the stars, who noticed that their remoteness was at one with the remoteness of death.

"Tell us, comrade, about how they fired at your head?"

It was hard for you to imagine that head, which brought you out from the sterile philosophy that you learnt in Rue d'Ulm, which tried to restore justice and to bring order to the jungle, could fall from a bullet.

"What were you thinking about when the executioner took aim at your head? Who did you dream about? Were you thinking about a woman of this world? Tell us, you archetype of man, what did you say the moment that you hit the ground? You were smiling. That is what Miraille said. They lit olive branches all over the world for you then. But what was the use?"

At night crows flew from a northern country to perch on the bars of the window. They caw in anticipation of your appointed hour. Once you cried out in complaint, and countless obstacles sprang up in your head. Let revolution be that spectre. You were longing for the elm and ash trees by the walls of deserted graveyards. Primeval. Red mixed with green. You produced many sentences for your notebooks. You tried to draw your future in them. But what future was there for you, prisoner? Oblivion and the daily routine of pain. Charming harmony of everlasting torture. Secret pain until the end. Everything around you was penitent. In exile, the ghosts came to you. Your masters: Marx, Nietzsche, Heidegger, the Republic of Shadows. That is how you spent subsequent years, planting words and harvesting the woman who came to you from afar seeking to wrench you out of that nothingness. The day you inspected your arms, your chest, your neck, and you found them all in their place, you were happy because you were still alive.

You, who used to try to shed some light on his past wondering. What made you go on living was the desire to be a father. You said this to your comrades when you were out of prison, and they found nothing treasonable or surprising in that. It had all been said before by prisoners. Transparent, like the face of your friend when you were in the jungle. The habits which produced the love in every night of your lives. Every shot was a straight line towards the construction of revolution and social justice. But what you needed after that was self-protection. Awake or unconscious, time had succeeded in scuppering desire. Neither today nor tomorrow was the moment for hunting hatred and injustice. A triumph over slavery? But you already knew that . . . Perhaps the irons were broken slowly. "The Revolution Within" and you claim to have created a new world. Hoping for a better world which never dies, where prisoners stand up to torture and do not divulge every secret they know or the names of their comrades outside the prison walls. Their bodies will remain tattooed with love for ever and their lives will turn into an endless celebration.

He sighed deeply. He took out his diary. He thought about writing a Song of Songs, the greatest love poem to Nadia, and to the revolution which had abandoned him. He thought about trying to be with her now under the lights of Ayntab. Paris asking questions. Paris awaiting the election results. Michel attacking François. Then everyone goes off to spend the weekend at their homes in the country. Olivier will make another film about the blueness of the sea and the greenness of the trees. Miraille will talk to him at length about her psychiatrist with whom she is discussing the moment of consciousness and unconsciousness. Here, everything falls apart. Everything falls into triviality and cosiness, right down to the long, overheated underground tunnels which penetrate Paris. Light is exiled in the darkness of the bombs fired far from this land. Bullets are fired at hearts. Political prisoners have their nails pulled out and their eyes plucked from their heads. Why does the world not return to purity? Why doesn't someone take history outside and screw it.

He took a blank piece of paper and wrote:

"I am unable to live amongst you. One day I hope to create light in the world. I leave you like the stones of argument and luxury in your beds. Win if you so desire."

He folded the paper calmly and walked to the door of the café. He threw one last glance at the faces of the regular customers. As he crossed the street, he thought about the time and the date: 10.00 am, September 1977.

Silence hung over Paris. It afforded the city an instant of death. What was he doing in this city? Would he give it a new birth?

Paris has become sterile after bringing so many children into the world. Now she is in her dotage. Is it really she who threw his personal happiness far away from her soil? He would return to her again, perhaps when age had turned her hair completely white.

He got into his car and turned on the ignition. He waited a few minutes before deciding where to go. Instead of heading towards Rue Bourbon-le-Château, he decided, on the spur of the moment, to turn the car around and go back to Orly Airport.

Paris and the cold morning ran away behind him. On the airport road, behind the houses of the little villages scattered along it, he could see another horizon. It was the colour of the sea. His eyes did not stray from his destination: the airport. From there he would pass over the conflagrations of the world.

Everything around him seemed to contain peaceful, unseen tunes.

When we sing of the time of cherries.
Gaiety of birds and the mockery of the nightingale.
They will all be here,
Terror in their eyes and madness in their heads.
Fighters. Lovers.
The sun in their hearts.
When we sing in the time of cherries,
The birds will live in a better way.

The plane was going to the East. His face was fixed on the clouds below him. How would he find her? Perhaps she had been consumed in the flames. He must be patient and carry with him a god-like desire, a desire to explain the nothingness of death. How helpless he was. How helpless he was without her. Without her he could not even live. He built up life, destroyed it, built it up again. The love of a woman fighter means complete supremacy over freedom. It is ultimate life in the blue depths.

He is travelling to her, unrestrainedly desiring to escape to her. Union with a body which does not bear the mark of a bullet is but a mute expression, nothing more than thin air. The body and the revolution merge together, become the natural intermediary between father and son.

Let him say goodbye to Europe, to the bosom of Europe, and her leaders. Let him leave it all behind, the metro stations, the adverts for Nestlé milk and Chantelle lingerie. He would fire new bullets at silence in the factory towns. His struggle will not come to an end this time. Nadia will be his absolute freedom and he will learn in her body the meaning of faithfulness towards death and life, before old age, before dotage. He will become the man of chivalry who neither deserts nor betrays.

"What we knew was love. But I didn't really know you nor you me, that's why you didn't yearn for me. Remember the first meeting. How can something so banal produce such an ending. Remember the burning desire to change into comets."

The aeroplane was getting closer to the East. The houses of Athens have small fires.

"You told me in the rain, on the Pont Neuf, the story of your first encounter with love. You lowered your voice and blushed."

The aeroplane approaches the East. The silence of the passengers whispers incomprehensibly. It turns to cacophony. In his eyes the Mediterranean below seems like a blue legend touching the sky.

He lifted his hand to his forehead and spent a moment in prayer, before the onset of battle. He remembered the first words that he had learnt there in the hot country. A burning memory of slain comrades rose from his heart and tore the deep inner night of his loneliness. The homelands are far apart and scattered, and now he was approaching a new homeland. He hears his heart beating. It was a sound he had ignored for a long time while he was going backwards and forwards between the Place de Dauphine and his party headquarters.

This time his wings were no longer just wings, they were the world.

Hamida Na'na
❀

Hamida Na'na was born in Syria. She graduated from Damascus University in 1971 and worked as a journalist before travelling to France to continue her education in literature and Islamic studies. She then worked for UNESCO between 1974 and 1977. During her subsequent appointment as head of the Europe and North Africa bureau at *Al-Safir* newspaper she published *Debates with Western Thinkers*, a series of interviews conducted with prominent writers such as Michel Foucault, Roland Barthes and Simone de Beauvoir. Her other novel *Man Yajrou 'ala al-Shawq* was published in 1989 and has recently been translated into German. Hamida Na'na currently lives in Paris and works for the monthly French magazine *Le Nouvel Afrique-Asie*.

Fadia Faqir
❀

Fadia Faqir was born in Jordan in 1956. She gained her BA in English Literature, MA in creative writing, and doctorate in critical and creative writing at Jordan University, Lancaster University and East Anglia University respectively. Her first novel, *Nisanit*, was published by Penguin in 1988 and her second novel, *Pillars of Salt*, is forthcoming. Fadia Faqir is a lecturer in Arabic language and literature at the Centre for Middle Eastern and Islamic Studies, Durham University. She is at present working on her third novel, *The Black Iris Crossing*.

Martin Asser
❀

Martin Asser is a freelance translator and Arabist living in London.